2

OTHER BOOKS BY SUZANNE HUDSON

In a Temple of Trees
In the Dark of the Moon

All the Way to Memphis

All the Way to Memphis

AND OTHER STORIES BY SUZANNE HUDSON

RIVER'S EDGE
— MEDIA —

Little Rock, Arkansas

2014

This is a work of fiction. All characters, organizations and
events portrayed in this novel are either products of the author's
imagination or are used fictitiously.

ALL THE WAY TO MEMPHIS: And Other Stories

by Suzanne Hudson

Copyright © 2014 by Suzanne Hudson

www.RiversEdgeMedia.com

Published by River's Edge Media, LLC
100 Morgan Keegan Drive, Ste. 305
Little Rock, AR 72202

Edited by Wendy Reed
Design by Paula Guajardo

Manufactured in the United States of America.

ISBN-13: 978-1-940595-03-0

For Madison and Melanie

TABLE OF CONTENTS

Acknowledgments

She is the best among us. Suzanne Hudson's new collection is cause for celebration; it brings together some of the finest short stories written in the South in the last decade or so. It is anchored by her story "Opposable Thumbs," which is fast becoming, like O'Connor's "A Good Man is Hard To Find" and Welty's "Why I Live At The P. O," a Southern classic, with its unforgettable opening line: "Kansas Lacey was twelve years old the summer Leo Tolbert carelessly took up a sharp hatchet, chopped off his five-year-old brother Cooter's thumb, and threw it up on the sloping tin roof of the jailhouse." The story was the title story of Hudson's first published book, a collection of short fiction published twelve years ago by the remarkable editor Joe Taylor at Livingston Press, the house that has been—in recent years—the springboard for a large number of the most original writers we have. Taylor has a real knack for uncovering innovative literary talent, and Suzanne Hudson is one of his prize discoveries. Since the appearance of her first book she has published two acclaimed novels, *In a Temple of Trees* and *In the Dark of the Moon*.

Hudson is an uncompromising and tenacious writer, never averting her eyes from the most disturbing and painful aspects of life. She—like O'Connor and Welty before her—often focuses on that stratum of our Southern culture that is at once its most alive and its most profane: the illusory world of rootless young women hanging out in honkytonks desperately looking for love; the very poor, eking out their lives in their forlorn, despairing poverty; children growing up in a world that is both cruel and sex haunted; the conflicts of family, its deepest felt bonds and its most explosive and passionate brutality: sexual abuse and domestic violence. These subjects are not easy to face or to write about, but Hudson does so with empathy and grace, because they are a significant part of her vision of the human condition.

Hudson's prose is lyrical and fluid. Her choices of detail are always accurate and dead-on; she writes like a tarnished angel. But the thing that most distinguishes her fiction is its abiding humanity. The people in these stories are fully alive, knowable—through the pen of this gifted writer—as they rise from the page and establish their palpable existence as warm and breathing beings, as real as the people you know and see every day, that you went to high school with, that you had a beer with last night at The Palomino Lounge. You know these people, and you are privileged to spend time with them, no matter how difficult they can be. Because never does Hudson not find their common humanity, their dignity, their truth.

That is, after all, what good fiction is, what it does. It's a celebration of life. It allows us to live within the skin of others, to see with their eyes, to experience what they feel, and thus our own limited lives are expanded for a few moments and we, too, are more fully alive. Hudson's honesty makes her fiction an extremely moral one; there are no false notes, no superficialities, nothing cute or sentimental. She is a courageous writer, not afraid of life in any of its manifestations. Like her character Savannah in "All The Way to Memphis," Hudson was "born without a filter," and for that fact every one of us who loves truly empathic and virtuous fiction can be eternally grateful.

William Cobb
Montevallo, Alabama
March, 2014

"Memphis, Home of Elvis and the ancient Greeks."
—Talking Heads

Opposable Thumbs

Kansas Lacey was twelve years old the summer Leo Tolbert carelessly took up a sharp hatchet, chopped off his five-year-old brother Cooter's thumb, and threw it up on the sloping tin roof of the jailhouse. Over the sweltering days that followed, Kansas, Leo, and his twin sister Roxy watched the tiny appendage go from orange to blue-green to black against hot silver, swirling small currents and sprinklings of decaying scents down to the scrubby back yard of the Blackshear County Jail. It was on a Thursday. It was 1962.

Leo was the jailer's boy, pudgy, pork-fed, and red-headed with freckles all over; Roxy was more angular, rust-haired and speckle-flecked as well, but pretty to Leo's plain. They lived in the house attached to the front of the jail, a dungeonesque Victorian structure with steep brick stairs and dark, barred windows that glared down at the back yards and alleys where they played. Victor Tolbert, the jailer, spent his days visiting a cold-edged humor on the inmates he kept, sometimes turning hard taunts at his wife, Joleen. When this happened and when stabbing words or the muffled pounding of a fist to a wall drifted from the open windows of the front rooms, the Tolbert children scurried like mice to Kansas's yard to create games and stay out of their daddy's way.

Next to the jailhouse was the office of the *Sumner Local*, serving the small town with church notes, wedding pieces, and farm news. Next to it was Kansas's grandparents' and great-grandmother's house, where Kansas had lived for the seven years since her mother's death.

The Lacey home stood crisp and white, jalousied windows across its face, looking out over the main street of town. Across the side alley, the courthouse loomed like the Acropolis, its huge domed clock chiming out the increments of childhood in surreal crescendos of hours and half-hours building to sultry noons and coarse midnights.

✳

The day of the thumb-chopping, Kansas spent the morning helping Great-Grandemona and LittleBit, the cook, make dinner for her grandfather and the prisoners. When Kansas had been orphaned at five, she had desperately insisted on calling her grandfather "Daddy."

"It's Grandfather," his wife, Miss Pearl, would correct her.

"Daddy," Kansas would stubbornly volley.

"Grandfather," came the return, until the bastardized moniker finally stuck, becoming ingrained in the fabric of the familial landscape.

Daddy would walk over from his office at the courthouse every day with the twelve o'clock chimes to have dinner with Kansas, Grandemona, and Miss Pearl. The dining room table would be set with silver and starched linen in his honor, and dotted with dishes of barefoot LittleBit's ham-juiced, fatback cooking, and syrupy sweet tea. After dinner, the ritual would move to the living room, where Daddy would knock back a shot of Early Times, then savor a second shot, slowly, inhaling a Camel as he watched the midday news on the TV. After a fifteen-minute nap, he would walk back over to the sheriff's office, leaving his wife to her soaps and peach brandy.

Kansas stirred the amber liquid in the yellow ceramic pitcher, the wooden spoon clicking at ice cubes. "Our prisoners sure do eat good, don't they? Mr. Hooker over at the hardware store says they ought to get bread and water is all." She dipped her little finger into the liquid and sucked a sugary drop from the improvised teat.

Grandemona's deft white hands carved at a tomato, unwinding its skin into one languid serpentine strand. "Anybody can wind up in a jail," she said. "Imagine if it was one of your people. Cane Hooker is just a mean old man."

"I can never get skins off in one piece," Kansas said, watching the red-orange tomato strip coil snake-like on the white metal tabletop as her Grandemona slid the tiny paring knife between skin and meaty pulp. The old woman twirled the fruit between thumb and palm as she peeled, mucus-pouched seeds sliding across her thumbnail. "You will with practice."

Kansas walked over to the sink and looked out over the back yard to where coal-black Pruella sat on the porch of Pinky's shotgun house, fanning herself with a cardboard funeral parlor fan. Both LittleBit and her sister Pruella now lived in the Quarter across the railroad tracks, but they had grown up in the Laceys' backyard. Their mother Pinky had been nursemaid to Miss Pearl, to Kansas's mother Ruby, and to Kansas herself for a time. Now she lay dying of cancer, so her daughters took turns staying with her. Kansas would sneak and visit her, too, even though her grandmother did not want her entering colored folks' houses. Not anymore.

Visiting Pinky had been just fine when she was five, her mother freshly packed beneath fertile South Georgia soil. In fact, Pinky's granddaughter, Bernice, was her primary childhood playmate, giggling with her at tea parties held on rainy days underneath Pinky's house, where they exchanged doll-babies of opposite hues. But Miss Pearl no longer welcomed Bernice once Kansas turned ten.

✳

Kansas's kinship with Pinky grew out of penetrating black nights in the aftermath of her mother's death, when Kansas crept from the big house to Pinky's bed, nestling against the old woman's flannel gown in a curled, soothing sleep.

"You ingrown, child. Ingrown like a toenail, into me," Pinky would laugh, "because I tended your mama, all through her growing up, put my soul into her when she just a baby. Then her soul go into you. Miss Pearl always be a cold woman; now she cold and lifeless, too, since her baby be dead. You come to Pinky when you want the truth. Pinky can't lie."

And Kansas did seek Pinky's truth over the years, the implicit understanding between them that their shared truth was not to be undressed before the family, mired as her folks were in ritual and propriety.

"Why do you reckon Mama killed herself?" Kansas asked in her eighth summer. She and Pinky sat at the metal table in Pinky's tiny kitchen, no wall separating it from the rest of the miniature house. Butter beans thumped into aluminum pots as they splayed the green sheaths, zipping thumbnails through thin, moist membranes.

"She took a fit is all," was the matter-of-fact reply. "She were always one or the other. High up in the trees or low down on the floor. She put that rope round her neck when she down on the floor. Just couldn't stand what all come behind her dealings with your daddy."

"Tell that part of the story," Kansas had urged, biting on a raw butter bean, sending a waxy singe to the back of her tongue.

"Yes, Lord. Your mama-Ruby thought Eddie Frye was about the handsomest thing on the world. He give you that dark hair of yours. He were a traveling salesman she met over to the Bye and Bye Club in Albany. From Topeka, Kansas, your daddy was."

"And that's how I got my name," the girl recited.

"Only cause your mama sneaked it up on her Daddy, is how."

"Sneaked it?" This was a new part of the story, and Kansas's ears tingled with curiosity.

"Yes, Lord. Your sneakin'-around mama went and sneaked you a name." Pinky fumbled through the butterbeans to find those still sheathed and hiding on the bottom of the pot, lying low beneath fallen kin.

"Sneaked how?"

"Well, when your mama told that Eddie Frye she were

with child, he cut and run. He weren't a damn bit of good, just like I knew. He left some hurt folks in Blackshear County, hurt to the bone. Your Daddy had all the deputy sheriffs and state police from here to Dothan chasing him down. They got him this side of the Chattahoochee. They must have worked him over real good, too, cause that handsome face of his was sure enough swole up when they brought him back. Took him to the courthouse with a cocked shotgun to his head. Had him say 'I do' and then run him straight back out of town again." She took the pot of beans to the rust-stained sink and began rinsing them.

"But what about the name?" Kansas reminded her.

"Oh. Miss Ruby's daddy say the courthouse wedding made you legitimate—not a bastard child—but the sorry name of Eddie Frye weren't good enough for his grandchild. That's why you took the Lacey name. Then, when you was birthed and your mama say, 'I think I'm going to call her Kansas,' Daddy went on and on about what a pretty name it was. I don't reckon he knew where that man was from and don't still to this day."

And Kansas wrapped herself within the folds of this one sharp secret, watching her features in mirrors over the years for the developing imprint of her no-good daddy—the olive skin, brown eyes, and ink-black hair that lived in her mother's last thoughts, as she swung gently from a pine limb near Scratchy Branch.

✻

Kansas vaulted herself to the countertop where she sat by the eight-eyed, double-ovened gas stove watching LittleBit stir corn meal and water in a thick mixing bowl. "Did you know," she said, "that you'd have an awful time stirring and Grandemona peeling if y'all didn't have opposable thumbs? I read it in *National Geographic*."

"You a reading somebody," LittleBit said.

"It's true," Kansas went on. "When the monkeys and all sprouted a thumb, it got to where they could peel food like bananas and open nuts and all kinds of other things. And just look at us humans. When the apes turned to cave men and our brains got big, we could do all sorts of stuff, like art, because of our thumbs."

"You saying we come from apes?" LittleBit asked sharply.

"'Cause that's evil talk." She poured the corn meal mixture into a flat iron skillet over a gas flame. Then she placed a large kitchen match between her teeth to suck up the stinging fumes of the white onion her knife pierced.

Kansas wiggled and curled the fingers of both hands into each other, then apart, then close to the eyes of LittleBit, who swatted them away. "Look how beautiful they are," Kansas insisted. She cupped them together in a gesture of prayer. "The Methodist preacher says God's hand hath wrought the Creation. Well I say the human hand hath wrought even more. Like the cathedral at Aachen. I saw it in *National Geographic*, too. Those Germans are some building folks."

"You go on, now," LittleBit turned the corn meal pie in the skillet. "Done wrought a mess," she muttered.

"Kansas, stop talking in riddles and don't contradict Brother Altman," Grandemona ordered.

"Yes'm." Kansas again looked out the window. Pruella had gone back inside the shack. The courthouse clock struck eleven-thirty.

"Yonder comes Sampson," Grandemona said as LittleBit placed triangles of hoecake into the tins that the trusty would carry over to the jail on large, stacking trays. Today there were nine tins of snap beans, fried chicken and mashed potatoes. The squeal and smack of the screen door and a rhythmic jangling of steel keys up the hall to the kitchen announced a short, stocky man, the color of an aging copper penny. He lifted the trays as they exchanged brief pleasantries.

"I'm going with him," Kansas announced, following the man in the white pants, a black stripe running up the outside of either leg. Then she thought to add, "Don't tell Miss Pearl."

As Kansas passed through puberty, Miss Pearl was less inclined to allow her to roam the jailhouse as she had in childhood. And it was common knowledge that her grandmother judged the Tolberts to be pure trash, so sometimes she did not even want Kansas playing in the jailhouse yard. "But they are the only children nearby," she would sigh. "Well, at least they are white."

"You be back by noon," Grandemona called after her.

Kansas knew not to talk to Sampson, though she had done enough of it over the months to learn that he was in jail for stealing a car, that his wife was a friend of LittleBit's, and that he spent most of his time washing Daddy's sheriff car or doing yard work around the jail or the courthouse. He spoke with a soft, muffly voice, and didn't seem like a thief when he warned the prisoners not to cuss or talk nasty around Kansas.

She followed him past Grandemona's flower garden and the big-leafed bouquet of a fig tree that Kansas often hid beneath, peering out at her world, at Pinky's house, enveloped in the harsh smell of sun-dappled black dirt and juices of roly-poly bugs and rotten figs. In the fecund cave formed by the fig tree, Kansas would marvel at the notion of Grandemona turning the hard, velvety-skinned fruit into shimmering preserves that wetly sugared LittleBit's buttermilk biscuits.

Today Leo was at the tree stump behind the jail with a hatchet, passing the time hacking sticks into smaller sticks, destroying things the way only boys could. Cooter sat in the dirt, picking at scabbed-over mosquito bites, tempting impetigo. Roxy was nowhere in sight, probably inside reading a Cheryl Ames, R.N., novel, feeding her interest in all things medical. She had read *Not as a Stranger* four times already this summer.

Once, she and Roxy had hidden beneath the fig tree in a night game of hide-and-seek with Leo. The two girls crouched motionless, muddy-toed and sliding sweat, for a short forever; thighs, shoulders, forearms touching and electric, shallow breaths filling the dampness with summer. Roxy's deep-red hair caught slips of moonglow oozing between the leaves, her eyes wide with childish fear, and Kansas suddenly wanted to kiss her. She leaned in, imperceptibly, drawn to the lips that panted swift currents in and out, under the shield of midnight green. When she was close enough to see, even in the earthen darkness, Roxy's front teeth gently working her lower lip the way she always did when she was nervous, Leo screamed. He snatched back a limb to expose them, making Kansas feel naked and ashamed of the mystifying urges taking her to places she dared not share with anyone, not even Pinky.

Kansas followed Sampson into the jail, the six-inch skeleton key making hollow clicks and rattles in the metal locks. They walked down a corridor of cells, the concrete floor stained with years of tobacco juice, amber imprints of time served, prisoners' voices echoing across the divide to one another. Each cell door had a rectangular port in the bars large enough to pass through the meal tins, and Sampson always let Kansas deliver them.

"Mmmmmm. I smell me some fried bird," the one called Joseph said.

Another one, called Gabe, said, "Tell Miss LittleBit she sure do some fine cooking. I'm going to send my wife by to get her recipe for hoecake."

And they all thanked her and didn't seem like criminals at all.

White prisoners were put on the far end of the corridor, but there were no white prisoners today. There was, however, a woman prisoner on the second-floor corridor whom Kansas did not want to see. Her name was Angel and she had been in the county jail for five months already, charged with attempted murder for dousing her husband with gasoline and setting him afire. Both of them had been badly burned, and one side of Angel's face and both hands and forearms were grotesquely scarred.

Kansas had only taken Angel's meal to her once, whistling her way up the narrow steps to a cell stacked with packs of Alpine cigarettes and movie magazines, where its occupant sat and puffed the days away to the dazzling lives of the stars. Angel had not praised the food or thanked anyone; she only looked at Kansas with her one good eye, the other draped in scarred flesh scythed like slick satin across the mahogany face.

"A whistlin' woman and a crowin' hen be sure to come to no good end," Angel had recited, her eye finding secrets in the skinny white girl bearing food.

Kansas had been ashamed and afraid to return. So when Sampson headed up the steps with Angel's tray, Kansas went out to where Leo was still producing piles of sticks with his hatchet.

"You are one big, sure-enough time waster," Kansas said, as the hatchet came down with another loud thwack.

"I'm going to build a fort for my army men," he said, indicating two cellophane bags of soldiers, Confederate and Union, battle flags and artillery lined up across the ash-gray dirt. "Go on, Cooter," he said to his little brother, who laid his hand on the chopping stump and drew it away in a taunt.

"Cooter, quit!" Leo demanded.

But Cooter repeated the motion as the hatchet came down, before Leo's brain registered it, and the thwack reverberated with the pained shriek of the child and Kansas's scream of revulsion.

The child lay writhing on the ground, squalling an ear-piercing wail, clutching his bloodied fist. Leo could only move slowly toward the chopping stump, repeating a mantra of "Don't tell Daddy, don't tell Daddy, don't tell Daddy." Suddenly, with a rush of nerve, he picked up the amputated digit and hurled it blindly as far and as hard as he could. Then he bolted, never looking back.

A crash of iron announced Sampson, jingling and clanking from the jailhouse. He pulled off his tee shirt and scooped the boy up just as Mrs. Tolbert and Roxy rounded the side of the building. Kansas could only stagger, heaving through the chain-link gate, horrified by a gore—the like of which she had never before witnessed. The leaves of the fig tree slapped at her face and arm as she passed, bound for her own back door, above which an industrial kitchen fan blasted a typhoon of noontime smells into the August heat.

✳

Miss Pearl sat tall at the dining room table, attentive only to Daddy, her husband since she was fifteen. She was a remote, delicate woman who barely haunted the house where Kansas grew up. She sipped peach brandy in the early afternoons and spent days at a time in bed, yet always appeared for meals. "She hasn't been the same since your mama died" was all Kansas ever heard by way of explanation, so her faint presence was accepted, and everyone, including her family, referred to her as "Miss Pearl."

"The nigrahs over in Albany are getting all tore up," Daddy was saying. "It's likely there'll be some trouble downtown this weekend. State police'll be there. Our office is to be on call."

"Why anybody would want to go where they aren't wanted I'll never understand," Miss Pearl said to her husband. "I wouldn't go within a mile of where I wasn't wanted."

"It's a damn mess, is all," Daddy said.

"You can't believe how Cooter hollered when Leo chopped his thumb off," Kansas said. "There was blood all over—"

"Not at the dinner table," Grandemona interjected.

"Yes'm."

"It's the goddamn federal government taking over how we do things," Daddy said.

"Thank goodness the nigrahs in Sumner don't carry on that way," Miss Pearl said.

Kansas thought about Pinky, how she used to keep her money folded in her sock and a can of snuff deep in her bra. Her skin was like black leather; her arms must have been sinewy and sure as they held the Lacey babies she had tended alongside her own.

"What would be wrong with Pinky or LittleBit going to the Walgreen's for a CoCola, Daddy?" Kansas asked.

"Kansas!" Miss Pearl hissed.

But Daddy was laughing. "It's a lot more complicated than that, and it's something you don't have to worry about. But if it's thumbs you want to know about, just ask Royce over at my office to show you the one he's got. Keeps it in a jar of alcohol down in his desk drawer. I'm surprised you've never seen it."

"That is enough," Grandemona snapped, "about body parts and race relations. I want a civilized conversation at my dinner table."

The exhaust fan in the kitchen hummed deeply to the swish-swishing as LittleBit scrubbed pots. The grown-ups chatted an effortlessly empty chat, but all the while Kansas felt awed by the happenstance appearance of two severed thumbs in the midst of her thirteenth summer.

✳

Royce Fitzhugh grinned as he held the small jar up to his desk lamp, Leo, Roxy and Kansas mesmerized by the gherkin-sized object floating in the chemical wash. The sheriff's office in and of itself was a mysteriously fascinating place. Kansas spent storm-gusty summer afternoons poring over the Wanted files and photographs of dangerous criminals, talking to state troopers riding the southwest Georgia highways, creating patterns of numbers on the ciphering machine, or typing notes to Leo and Roxy on the big black Royal typewriter on Daddy's desk.

Every great once in a while, she would talk Daddy into opening up the evidence closet to show her guns, knives, and tire irons, instruments of assaults and occasional murders being tried in the upstairs courtroom. Once he had let her sample a sip of shinny that had been tested clean by state experts; it ran a trail of fire down her throat, sending her coughing and gagging out to the water fountain in the cavernous hallway. "Whites Only" the sign above the fountain had said, and she was grateful at that moment to be white.

"I got it from Victor Tolbert, your very own daddy," he said to Leo. "Vic said he found it in a fox trap, like some poor fellow had a tragic accident, kind of like Cooter, I hear."

Leo looked down sheepishly.

"Can I hold the jar?" Kansas asked.

"Sure thing, girl," Royce grinned.

It was translucent almost, veins and muscle like dwarfed spaghetti tubes inside the larger tube of the thumb, lightly spotted in places like some strange bruised fruit. The thumbnail had settled on the bottom of the jar, but the place it had once grown upon was definable, and Kansas felt a shudder rip through her as she realized there had been an actual person attached to this tiny bit of flesh and bone.

Royce laughed. "You got to have a stomach for it, I reckon.

But a sweet little girl like you ain't never got to worry over seeing such as this."

"I'm going to be a doctor," Roxy said, "so I'll see dead people all the time."

Royce laughed harder. "Ain't no such of a thing."

"She will, too," Kansas insisted. "She's going to Emory and be a baby doctor."

The deputy chuckled them out the door. "Ain't no girl going to be no doctor. Especially not no jailer's girl. Get on, now."

Two curved wooden staircases led up to the courtroom, where they regularly played Perry Mason, acting out bizarre murder trials concocted from the thick summer air. The trio sat on the bottom step.

"Where's Cooter's thumb?" Roxy asked. "I want to cut it open and see what's inside." The younger boy was still at the hospital in Albany, his parents yet to come home; Sampson was in charge of the jailhouse.

"Don't know," Leo said, glancing a warning at Kansas.

"I looked all around the chopping stump. It would've been there, so don't be stupid. Kansas?"

Kansas spread out her hands and shrugged. "Maybe a squirrel ate it," she offered.

"Daddy's going to be mad as hell," Roxy said. "I'm just trying to help you." She gazed into her brother's brown eyes, her gold-flecked ones looking deeper until he buckled.

"I was scared of what Daddy would do, so I threw it away. I don't know where."

"You thought you could cover the whole thing up?" Roxy's eyes grew larger. "Are you a retard?"

"He panicked, is all," Kansas said. "Let's go hunt the

thumb."

The grounds of the courthouse were greenly manicured, sidewalks bordered with monkey grass. At the northwest and southeast diagonal corners of the lawn were steps leading down to recessed toilet areas for coloreds. Leo spat into the stairwell as they walked past it. "Nigger shit," he mumbled.

It was only after a half-hour search of the back yard of the jailhouse that Kansas caught the glint of the sunset on the high tin roof of the jail. The thumb lay where it had been pitched. They could make out the meaty end bearing blackened blood, and reasoned that it must be wedged on a bent nail or a stob in the tin that prevented it from following gravity to the ground. They took an oath to keep its location a secret, to gather to view its decomposition each day, and to never tease Cooter about his missing thumb or make him feel freakish in any way.

✳

LittleBit sat in the dark on the porch of Pinky's shack, barefoot, smoking her Salem, a small lamp from a bedside table within drawing moths to the screen. Pruella had gone back across the tracks to see to her children; LittleBit, who had no children, only a husband long dead, now spent the nights with her dying mother. She wiped at her sweaty neck with her palm, and Kansas thought her face, light cocoa glazed with acorn-hued freckles, was unusually strong and beautiful.

"I'll sit with her if you want to walk over to the Blue Goose," Kansas said. She knew LittleBit liked to visit the club just across the tracks, come back all giggly with beer and flirtation.

"You'd better get on, before Miss Pearl sees you out here."

"It's okay. I told them Roxy and Leo and me were going on a playout. We go all over town on a playout, and I don't have to go in until Daddy turns on the siren."

The town that was their playground was a two-block-square expanse of narrow alleys and stone buildings: the Feed and Seed, the Five and Dime, Mason's Drug Store, Hooker's Hardware, and others that lined the streets, their granite faces inscrutable. The bank's front was shiny black marble, cool and rich; Dougie Moore's Furniture Store had swing sets and yard chairs along the sidewalk, their own private park. On summer evenings the three of them would do night dances across sidewalk fields of darting palmetto bugs and moribund cigarettes, finding adventures in store window displays, climbing the fire escape to the courtroom's open windows, filling it with new dramas.

"I won't be but a little while," LittleBit said as the wood steps groaned under her callused feet. Her thin yellow dress, held together at the waist with a safety pin, framed the sturdy form beneath it as she stepped through the hazy glow of a street lamp into the dimness on its other side.

✳

"I'll have me a shot now," Pinky said as Kansas entered.

"You hurting?"

"It's Satan's own fire," Pinky said.

Kansas opened the cigar box that held several syringes and vials, plus the mysterious white powder brought from Albany by a friend of Sampson's. Kansas smiled, thinking how jealous Roxy had been to know Kansas had a patient in her back yard. She held the spoon over a kitchen match until the liquid was ready. She tourniquetted Pinky's arm, then pricked the vial, drawing back the plunger, carefully, to the mark LittleBit and Pruella had shown her. The vein easily took the pop and gentle slide of the needle's point. Pinky's eyes rolled back, black lids falling almost the whole way, pulling her into an abbreviated sleep while a solemn cadence of crickets and humming bugs droned dirges in the dark.

✳

Kansas sat on the edge of Pinky's bed, the old woman just awake after a short drowse. Pinky was alert now, pain muffled enough for company, so Kansas launched into her tales of severed thumbs, the habits of the apes, and the trouble in Albany. When she turned to Pinky for a comment she drew back instinctively. The old woman's black eyes, expressive of a sudden shock, surrounded as they were by the dark circles of illness, gave her face the ghoulish look of a deep brown skull. Pinky reached out to touch her forearm.

"It's all right," she said. "It's only Pinky." She gave a deep sigh that caught in her neck and became a wrenching cough. She spat in a Maxwell House coffee tin she kept on the bedside table. "You done said a heap just now. And a heap more to come, I bet. You be wanting the truth, just ask. I won't be dying with a lie on my lips."

"Do you think it's wrong not to tell where Cooter's thumb is? So his mama can maybe bury it?" Kansas asked.

"No, baby. Cooter's thumb ain't got no spirit in it. It's just a old shell, just like the ones them biddies leaves in your Grandemona's chicken coop. Just like Pinky going to be real soon. 'Course, some of Cooter's spirit might be done leaked out of that hole in his hand before they got it all sewed up. But he'll be all right."

"Leo's mostly scared of what his daddy's going to do," Kansas said.

"Well, them children ought to be scared of they daddy. You stay slap away from him. He a evil somebody. He's done busted many a nigger's head, plus his woman's. And that girl child of his better be sly cause he humps the woman prisoners, white and colored."

Kansas's face grew hot at the reference to sexual intercourse, a term Roxy had once shared with her along with the stark details.

Pinky chuckled. "You old enough. Ain't no sense in keeping them thoughts away from Pinky. You be doin' it your ownself before too long."

"It's nasty!" Kansas spat out. Roxy had told her about the milky stuff that would fire out of the man's penis and into the woman.

"Well, it's how we all come to be," Pinky said. "It's how you come to be."

"How come LittleBit didn't do it with her husband?"

Pinky laughed with all the energy she could muster. "You don't get no baby every time. Folks do it 'cause they like it. You'll see one day."

They talked on for a while, Pinky allowing that the trouble in Albany was bound to come and right as rain, allowing that she liked doing it with her husband, even though he left her when LittleBit was born, allowing that she was not afraid to die. Kansas put out the light when Pinky finally slept again, just as LittleBit's bare soles slapped against the steps.

✳

Friday afternoon found Kansas, Leo, and Roxy sitting around the chopping stump gazing up at the thumb, still perched imperiously on the tin stob. It had not changed much, but it was quite high up; subtle colorations could not be noted yet. Cooter had come home during the morning but was to mend indoors for a few days lest he infect his stitches.

"I don't think Daddy and Miss Pearl do it," Kansas said, shuddering at the image.

"Sure they do," Roxy said. "All men do, anyway. Who else could he do it with?"

"I want to do it," Leo said. "And I will."

The courthouse clock chimed out four-thirty, sending droves of sparrows out from under the dome in a frenzied flapping.

"Y'all want to play out tonight?" Kansas asked.

"Sure." Leo drew circles in the dirt with one of his chopped sticks, the Civil War fort still only a vague intention. Kansas reached over and touched the swollen bruise on his left cheekbone with her fingertips.

"Does it hurt?"

"No."

"I can't play out at night anymore. Daddy thinks I'm off with boys," Roxy said.

"But that's crazy!" Kansas kicked at some of the sticks. "You're with us. We're your witnesses."

"Daddy says we're all liars," Roxy said.

"To hell with Daddy!" Leo strode across the yard and began banging at the chain-link fence with a baseball bat, sending rattling shocks all the way down its length.

Roxy gazed down at her hands, tucking her left thumb under as though imagining what Cooter's life might feel like from here on out. "It'll be strange," she said. "The three of us going to Blackshear County High School next month, being the youngest class. Seventh graders."

"You think any coloreds will ever try to come? Folks keep saying so."

"Not as long as my daddy has a gun, they won't." Leo had tired of bludgeoning the fence and joined back in the talk. "And I'll personally kill any nigger that thinks he's going to sit in a class with me." The rawness of his anger shoved itself into the words.

"Daddy feels the same way, I think," Kansas sighed. "I don't know, though."

Leo threw the bat hard into the fence. "I'm going to go look at Royce's thumb again," he called over his shoulder as he walked away.

"Do you think we'll stay friends?" Roxy asked, and her gold-flecked eyes were incredibly sad. "It's such a big school. All those older boys."

"Since when were you scared of anybody?" Kansas asked.

"Since forever." She stood. "I'll tell Leo to meet you at the fig tree at dark."

Kansas watched her step through the chain-link gate and walk up the side yard of the jailhouse, the afternoon sun playing the rich red of her hair beneath its glow into muted flames. She stopped abruptly at the corner of the front porch, took a deep breath and forged ahead, her delicate hands coiled into tense, knotted fists at her sides.

✳

"I want to show you something." Leo caught her hands, pulling her from where she sat beneath the fig leaves.

"What?"

"Just be quiet," he snapped. "And do what I say."

They crept through the dark that was just past dusk, toward the jailhouse yard.

"Where—" Kansas breathed.

"Shhh!" He motioned her to follow as he entered the back stairwell of the jail through the door that remained open during the summer's hottest heat. A few steps up to the first barred door, and the male prisoners' conversations hummed and lilted through the iron slats. Leo flattened his back against the opposite wall of the stairwell, easing up the brick steps. He put a finger to his lips and she followed his lead. The stairs zigged, then zagged toward the second floor. Just as they zagged she could hear it, a heavy, rhythmic, grunting exhalation as if one were being punched repeatedly in the stomach, and a slapping, sucking sound. She hesitated, but Leo clutched her wrist, eyes warning her not to cry out. The grunting came louder and quicker now. They stepped up the last increments of the bricks.

Angel's cell was angularly framed by the doorway, steel bars slashing the picture into six-inch segments. Yet the picture they saw was clear: Angel naked on her back on the unyielding bunk. Victor Tolbert on top of her, knees cocked, pounding into her with all his strength and speed, groaning raspy growls into her neck. And all the while, Angel's arm, draped over the side of the bunk, a burning cigarette clamped between two fingers, never lifted to her lips. And her one good eye, the other being scarred into blindness, riveted into a blank nothingness from an expressionless face.

When Leo and Kansas emerged from the jail, she punched him three times in the back with her fist and ran for Pinky's house, where the lights were unusually bright and a small knot of ladies from Pinky's church whispered to Pruella.

"Pinky gone, child," Pruella said gently. "Gone home to Jesus. LittleBit inside tending her."

Kansas gazed at a girl on the porch she knew to be the Bernice of her childhood, blood kin to Pinky. Kansas nodded and turned toward Miss Pearl's big white house, itself a crypt for the lifeless.

✳

On Saturday afternoon she watched the paddy wagons roll in from Albany, loaded down with black folks who sat down in the middle of the city because they wanted a CoCola. The county jail in Albany was packed, so the surrounding counties took on the overflow. Miss Pearl was worried that LittleBit wouldn't be able to find a cook to replace her as she mourned her mama, but LittleBit surprised them all by announcing she would spend the next few days, twenty-four hours per if need be, in the kitchen cooking for the Albany folks. Pinky would want her to, she said.

It was during that marathon cooking session in the Lacey kitchen, late in the evening when the family slept under humming air conditioners, that LittleBit told Kansas a story. It was about how her husband, Ned, went fishing up Scratchy Branch one warm autumn night some fourteen years earlier. It was only about a mile up the branch that he stumbled upon a white couple having sex on the bank, the glare of the moon against their skin turning them the color of catfish bellies. The man spied him before he could slip off and ran him down. By the time the rumor ran its course, the tale had LittleBit's husband deliberately sneaking up to watch, "just to see a naked white lady get her eyes fucked out," LittleBit said.

Ned went into thin air, but they found him a week later, strung up from a longleaf. Nobody was ever charged, and nobody ever took credit for it, but it was said to be Klan. Ned had been beaten, hanged, and castrated. Strangest of all, every one of his fingers and toes was missing, and some said they were passed out amongst the Klansmen as souvenirs. Meantime, the white man on the creek bank didn't have the decency to marry the white woman and save her reputation, even when, not long after, she turned up pregnant.

Kansas listened as Pinky's truth came full circle. Faint traces of her mother's anguish made futile stabs at her memory, but Kansas did not want to comprehend the rippled effects ringing her conception in the gravelly sand alongside Scratchy Branch. She thought of the shell of Pinky's body, lying out back in her tiny shotgun last night while LittleBit bathed her for the colored folks' undertaker. She wondered if the worn flannel gown was still in Pinky's bureau. There was no one to be ingrown with, and she dreaded what was to come.

She observed Cooter's thumb a few more times, perfunctorily, never looking Leo in the eye, unable to reveal the truth to Roxy. Then one day it was gone, perhaps carried off by a scavenging rat or an errant blue jay, so there was no longer the pretense of a reason to visit the jail yard. Instead, Kansas crouched beneath the fig tree for quarter-hours at a time, studying Pinky's empty house and Miss Pearl's equally empty one.

In the late afternoons leading to September, Leo, Kansas, and Roxy roamed Sumner's streets and alleys, kicking rocks and bottle caps into the silence growing between them, serenaded only by the chimes of the courthouse clock. One desolate Sunday, Kansas and Roxy put pennies on the railroad tracks, and, while a thundering string of freight cars mashed the money into thin copper puddles, Leo tossed slurs and track gravel toward the rows of shacks beyond the Blue Goose. The bank's black marble facade threw reflections of the three of them behind the Feed and Seed, Leo poking poultry corpses with a sharp stick, the girls shuddering at the odor of stale chicken droppings, feathered carcasses, and the decaying eggshells of newly-hatched biddies. And while Roxy hung back, shoulders hunched with a splintering spirit, Kansas stomped the mounds of shells with her bare feet. The drying embryonic spittle stuck bits of eggshells to the summer-toughened skin of her soles, and razor-thin shavings zipped stinging slices into the tender, untouched secrets between her toes.

Yes, Ginny

Ginny Widdamacher's stepdaddy, Johnny Lee Fowler, went missing sometime Christmas Day, though no one could be sure when. After all, there were friends and relatives in and out, gift-wrapped boxes blotting out some of the routine family scenes, ripped paper tearing sheared holes in the underlying goings-on of the place and its blurred boundaries. A spirited din of raucous voices and laughter buzzed through the holiday pretend play of the children in the ramshackle trailer.

Johnny Lee's absence was first mentioned around mid-afternoon, and the family was hard-pressed to remember when, exactly, they had last noticed him, passed out in his perpetually-worn purple and gold plaid pajamas. As always, the LSU cap was turned sideways on his head in a way that annoyed Ginny's mama to no end. Everyone agreed that he had spent at least some of Christmas Day there in the La-

Z-Boy recliner like the lump that he was, deaf and numb from the Old Charter. Ginny's relatives, a collective noun of arms and legs and faces, whose conversations writhed in and around one another's like reptilian snarls in a pit of stranded snakes, offered theory after theory about where Johnny Lee Fowler had got off to, suggesting such offerings as:

1. He went to the A&P to buy cigarettes and watch folks come in for batteries for their bawling kids' toys

2. He went to the bowling alley that never closed to drink and shoot pool with Pete and Bootie and Killer Jones, derelicts all, who were surely there, as they were every other day of the year, listening to Johnny Cash on the jukebox and swapping lies

3. He went to harass and romance Connie Babb, that skank of an ex-girlfriend of his, the one he went to prison over, for slicing her across the cheekbone with a switchblade knife

4. He went outside to take a leak and passed out in the woods

5. He went somewhere, anywhere, driving his muffler-loud Chevy, with a belly full of booze and an attitude, and got himself locked up, again

But Ginny, six years old and swept up in the magic of Christmas, didn't care where he was or where he might be. She didn't like Johnny Lee Fowler. He was mean to her mama and mean to her brothers and mean to her. He sat in her real daddy's burnt-orange recliner and yelled to be waited on by her mama, bossed her brothers to do their chores, and squint-watched her for the least little mistake so he could call her a doofus or a retard or a maggot-head. And when he got up from that chair, he staggered and stumbled and shoved and slapped and punched. Sometimes he fell out in the floor and the family would step over him as if he were not there, mouth gapped open, drooling saliva, a cigarette's dying glow clamped between his hairy knuckles. So Ginny was nothing but glad that he had disappeared.

She spent the day rearranging the cardboard furniture in her Barbie Dream House, making up pretend dramas with Barbie and Ken and Skipper: Skipper running away from home and becoming a trapeze artist; Barbie kissing Ken because he saved her from a thing kind of like The Blob; Barbie throwing furniture at Ken because he liked Skipper better than her. In between conjured-up dramas, she played languid games of Candy Land and Chutes and Ladders with her older brothers, bent the wrists and joints of her brothers' G.I. Joe dolls, and pretended to be a majorette in the uniform Santa Claus had brought her. The relatives spent the day cooking and talking and laughing and bickering and cursing and drinking and, later in the day, wondering, though only in spurts, just where the hell Johnny Lee Fowler was.

"That's a stupid damn thing," Johnny Lee had said to her, early that morning when the light was dim, his hang-over thick, when she ran her little-girl-smooth palm over the Dream House, awed and proud. "Ain't nothing but a cardboard box. And somebody's hand-me-down, too."

She didn't answer back. She never did. She already knew the Santa who visited her got his toys from the Fire Department. The Fire Department had a used toy drive every fall, toys they painted and repaired for the poor kids, the non-discriminating children they thought wouldn't notice a nick here or a ding there or a scratch underneath. When Ginny took one of her Santa presents, a Tiny Tears doll, to Show-and-Tell in kindergarten, another little girl, Glendaline Moorer, came up to her afterward and said, "That's my old doll I gave to the firemen. That right there's where I stuck push-pins in her leg." And she pointed to the scattering of bore holes, the pricked, pink-plastic flesh, the pattern of dots Ginny had already noticed, been suspicious of, and now had confirmed as the mark of a cast-off.

Less than a month later Johnny Lee Fowler moved in, loving on her mama, pretending to like Ginny and her brothers, doing little odd jobs around the trailer, calling their home a tin can and calling himself a stepdaddy. He worked at the paper mill until summer, when he claimed he hurt his back, then badgered Ginny's mama into quitting her job at the Ben Franklin and going to work at the mill herself, working the night shift, making better money, enough to barely pay the bills, but not enough to entice the Santa who delivered brand-new toys. That Santa visited the other side of the creek, where Glendaline Moorer lived, where the little girls wore shiny hair ribbons and pressed pinafores with white eyelet ruffles.

For his part, Johnny Lee collected a government check, every cent of which went to the liquor store in town or for Alpine cigarettes or for bets on games of pool, or, as her mother accused from time to time, for other women. He planted himself in the burnt-orange recliner and looked at the TV when he wasn't out with his running buddies. He ensconced himself in that recliner for hours on end, thumping cigarette ashes into the honey-colored glass receptacle on the TV tray at his right side, reaching for the bottle of amber liquid on the floor at his left, anchored to the spot by the whiskey and the fuzzy glow from the television screen. "Turn that damn hat around," her mama would say to him. But Johnny Lee just sneered, "Can't see the TV good enough with the bill out front," and the only time he turned his hat frontwards was when he made to leave the house. Ginny loved to see his hat turned frontwards.

Ginny and her brothers were allowed to sit in the living room with Johnny Lee in the evenings, in front of the television that glowed fantasies into the shabby little trailer home. They were not allowed to pick any programs, but watched whatever Johnny Lee Fowler wanted to watch—*The Ed Sullivan Show, Alfred Hitchcock Presents, Perry Mason, The Twilight Zone*—until he ordered them to bed. They knew not to argue, knew not to dispute or resist or offer up any evidence that they had anything like thoughts and feelings of their own.

Ginny shared a tiny room beside the bathroom with two of her four brothers, usually sleeping wedged against their calves and heels at the foot of the bed. Whenever she couldn't sleep, she listened to the night, to her brothers' snores, to the television until it signed off with the crescendoing strains of "The Star-Spangled Banner" and turned into hissing gray snow, to the uneven steps of Johnny Lee's bare soles against the linoleum as he stumbled for the bathroom, invading the dimness in the hall. She listened to the wall groan as he leaned his palm against its opposite side while he used the toilet, trickling his imprint into those spaces in the little trailer where her own wishes and dreams resided, and she began to wish on him, on his intrusion. She began to wish him away and into thin air, like that magician did the lady in the box on Ed Sullivan's show; she wished him broken down on the stand, like Perry Mason always did the bad guys; she wished him into a suspense-filled fantasy, into the twilight zone of no logical explanation. And all that wishing, it seemed, had all of a sudden paid off, because now, on Christmas Day, he had vanished.

As the afternoon dimmed, the relatives fretted and frothed and stewed and railed about that sorry Johnny Lee Fowler, to skip out on his family on such a day, to rise up out of his drunken wallow to go and do something else, something he deemed more important than the day Jesus was born. They demanded answers of his empty chair. What about the children? Wasn't this *their* day, the children's? Didn't he realize how disappointed the little ones were? But, most of all, wouldn't he catch it when he got back home! And they offered Ginny's mama advice and admonishments and ultimatums about how to adequately punish Johnny Lee for his holiday-season sins. They rolled their eyes and ate more turkey and drank more beer and vodka and gin and whiskey, while Ginny and her brothers played in their walled-off worlds of pretend, the living room a sprawl of toys and dime store candies and nuts and apples, the hot-bulbed lights on the four-foot-tall tree burning her brothers' skin whenever they wrestled each other into its artificial branches.

Ginny sashayed in her majorette uniform, though there were some frayed places along the hem. Every once in a while she would catch the pattern of Johnny Lee's purple and gold pajamas in the corner of her eye, see the sideways-turned LSU cap that made her mama so mad, and feel a small tickle of a shudder at the nape of her neck. She would cut her eyes to the place where his whisper of a presence tried to break through, seeing—nothing. So she dismissed the fear and grounded herself in imagination. Instead of worrying over the possibility of his return, she pretended to twirl the flaking silver baton, its marshmallow-knobs at the ends now dull from being dropped. She wished for white boots with big red tassels, just like the majorettes at the high school wore when they pranced out ahead of the marching band, which formed and re-formed itself into shapes as it marched, reconfiguring itself into a drum, a star, into loops and interlacing circles before dissolving into another set of lines, marching to the stands, leaving the field empty and green and waiting for the game to proceed.

After the sunlight died, the relatives drifted out into the night, back to their own homes. The friends, though, still came and went while her mama fumed and sighed and sobbed over where Johnny Lee might be. Had that slutty ex-girlfriend picked him up at the foot of the dirt road, out of the family's line of vision? How had he managed to slip through the crowd? Her mama blew her nose a lot and smoked cigarette after cigarette while her best friend cursed Johnny Lee Fowler for a low-life piece of nothing that meant nothing but misery. "But I love him," Ginny's mama said, as if that answered all arguments.

Her mama had loved Ginny's real daddy, too, even though he was not a nice man, either. Ginny had vague memories of a shotgun trained on them all, of her mother leaning over the sink while her busted nose bled a slick sheet of red to the porcelain, of her oldest brother screaming with the sting of a leather belt. She remembered wishing her daddy away, wishing him dead. And it had worked, when her daddy was killed in an automobile accident on Highway 59, exactly one summer before Johnny Lee took up with them.

Late that night, Ginny sat on the floor beside Barbie's Dream House, the heavy cardboard case open to reveal upstairs and downstairs rooms full of colorful, modern, clean-lined furniture, though the cardboard was bent in at a table corner here, torn on a chair leg there. She imagined Barbie as a beautiful majorette in a satin uniform, and marched the doll naked across the floor of the Dream House, Barbie's plastic feet perpetually arched for stilettos, black eyelashes forever swooped up solid, mounded breasts fixed, unmoving, and devoid of nipples. Barbie marched across the scatter of toys on the floor, to the beat of a marching song, and up and over the arm of the empty chair, then up and across its back to the other arm. "It's time to go to sleep, Virginia Anne," her mama slurred and sighed, laying her head down on her own arms as she sat at the kitchen table, while her best friend made a pot of coffee.

Ginny closed the Dream House—Barbie, Ken, Skipper, and all their furniture tucked away for the night—and stood, and stretched, and yawned, but as she turned to the hall, to go to bed with her brothers' calves and ankles, she noticed something very, very odd. It was something that certainly would have been noticed earlier, in all the uproar surrounding Johnny Lee's mysterious absence. It would have been noticed by now had it been present before now, but it seemed to have simply dropped from thin air, from a hole torn in the ether, from a place of no logical explanation.

It was a cap—the purple and gold LSU cap—the one he wore always, turned to the side for TV and to the front for leaving. At this moment it was turned to the front, in the very middle of the seat of the La-Z-Boy recliner. Ginny walked over to the burnt-orange chair, eyes wide, full of the kind of astonished surprise brought by Christmas gifts anticipated in dreams but not truly expected in reality. She picked up the cap, drawing in a breath, then set it back down and fingered the rough fabric that covered the chair, let her touch go to some of the places where a lit cigarette had left circles of melted black enmeshed in the material. There were burned marks on the TV table beside the chair as well, and a mound of butts in the honey-colored ashtray. The Old Charter bottle sat on the floor where he had left it, a strange sight to see it left there, as the bottle always went wherever Johnny Lee went. Ginny nudged it with her big toe, sliding it closer to the chair, smiling, gazing at the empty chair, at where the indentation of him was still pressed into the coarse, rumply upholstery.

She turned, but, one more time, in the corner of her eye, came the pattern of plaid that was him, there in the dented foam where his body had born down, where the LSU cap now sat, facing front. She leaned close, and still closer to the cushioned seat where he had lounged, day in and day out, barking insults, picking at weaknesses, stick-poking at hidden angers, cementing insecurities. She looked into the weave of the fabric, deep into the threads loomed into one another, and a separate weave began to emerge. She squinted, adjusted, aligned her vision. There it was. There, within the pattern of burnt-orange, the solid color of the chair, came another color, then another, as a new pattern emerged, though melded deep within the recliner's thick covering. It was the purple and gold plaid of his pajamas, forever imbedded in the depths of that chair, the place where, in selfish ignorance, he strode on the edge of a lost child's reconfiguration, the transcendence of her dreams. Johnny Lee Fowler's presence had given Virginia a wish, and the ripening of that child's fresh wish had taken him into thin air, into the kind of forever where faith danced in the yellow satin slippers of sugar plum fairies.

The Thing With Feathers

She didn't meet her stepfather until she was five, having lived with a cousin of her mother's in Beaumont, Texas, since she was born, having been ensconced in the womb during the marriage ceremony. An apathetic judge of probate oversaw the wedding, a hasty, desperate ritual her mother rushed at, in order to find legitimacy for herself and, by default, her daughter. In 1950, the world of small town Alabama did not look kindly upon unwed mothers, and her own mother thought it best to spend some time alone with this man who was now a husband, would be a husband for the next thirteen years, until he shot himself in the head on a creek bank—accidentally, some said; on purpose, said others.

The relative who brought her up to the age of five was sometimes affectionate but many times harsh, tugging at the child's clothing in frustration as she dressed her, brushing, too hard, at the tangles in the child's hair, impatient and full of spat-out sighs, like the sounds of an angry cat. Still, there were storybooks read in drowsy snuggles on the relative's bed when it was time for a nap. There were stories the relative told for truth, about God and Jesus and arks and healings; but mostly there were fairy tales: "Snow White and Rose Red," "Jack and the Beanstalk," "Rapunzel." The toddler, the child, did not understand all the words, the intricacies of plot, but the soothing sound of her surrogate mother's voice spun silky tendrils of hope, though she couldn't name it at the time, around her unclaimed heart.

Her mother visited her on her birthdays, sent her packages at Christmas time, doll babies in shiny wrapping paper tied up in fumbled ribbon, shipped in boxes all bumped and scarred by errant postmasters. The child played with the dolls in the floor of the relative's kitchen while boiling cabbage eked its humid, acrid scent into the walls, the curtains; cheap furniture disemboweling brown-flecked stuffings across the linoleum. Then one day she was told it was time to go and meet her stepfather.

She remembered hanging back, there in the doorway of her new parents' house, dropping her eyes from his overpowering form. He was all plaid flannel shirts, khaki work pants, and heavy boots that seemed to shake the earth, like the giant in "Jack and the Beanstalk." And he worked to win her over, his fingers nibbling at her ribs, games played until he drew her in to the fun he concocted, though she always glanced away, holding back a bit of herself. "She's shy," her mother said, but she wasn't. So he called her "Sugar Bugger" and "Baby Doll" and "Dipsey Doodle." When he came in from work he would throw her in the air and the world would blur and the colors would bleed into each other and she would shriek with delighted laughter, even though there was that quick moment of terror, breath sucked back and where was Jesus?

Her stepfather had a shotgun for killing deer, limp brown forms laid blood-spotted in the bed of his truck on autumn evenings. He had a thick-handled, thin-bladed silver knife for slitting through the skins of squirrels and catfish, or carving through the meat of an apple to offer her a small slice: "Eat it down, Sugar Bugger. An apple a day keeps the doctor away." He had a pistol he would use sometimes at night, to shoot at the raccoons that dug in the garbage, crashing her awake, sending her screaming and crying to her mother, who would say, "Don't be a silly girl. Go back to sleep. Your mama's tired as the devil."

He had a collection of fishing lures—rubber worms in purple and orange, golden spinners shimmering, enticing her—a kaleidoscope's colors, some like feathered jewels in the hinged, top-handled treasure chest he carried.

"Show me the thing with feathers, Daddy," she would say, for he had insisted, insisted that she call him "Daddy," and she, who had never had one, tried the word on and enjoyed the way the sound of it wrapped her in the feel of a safe-layered warmth.

"They ain't feathers," he would say, pulling out the shyster lure, letting her tickle it with the soft tips of her fingers. "Fish don't eat nothing with feathers."

He drank beer most of the time—like water, her mama said—and whiskey of an evening, and if the child was up too late, or lucky enough to be invited to sleep in the big bed next to her mama, she would sometimes see the other man emerge, the one who was much more unpredictable, the stumbling one, who mumbled curses and kicked her mother's bedroom door when she shut him out.

"Don't want no drunk slobbering over me," her mother would say.

He finally took her fishing when she was six, a special day, just the two of them, to a pond that pooled a blue stain in the woods, where he cast into the weeds, building a mound of empty cans, with each toss of a can a glance at her, going from strange into threatening into frightening and where was Jesus? Then, the pile of cans grown to maturity, when the sun caved in to the horizon, he twirled her hair around his fingers, stroked her face, her little arms without recourse because she didn't understand. And when he put his hand to her panties, the soft white cotton ones her mother hung out on the line each week to dry, the ones he would throw into the blue pond going all deep-colored as the sun withdrew, tears streaked trails of salt down her cheeks because it hurt and she wanted her mama.

In elementary school the child was not especially noticeable, moving at an average pace, producing average work, sometimes pushing at the rules, as children will do, seeming good-natured, even charming at times. She raised her hand, walked single file, clattered her green plastic tray along stainless steel bars in the lunch line, flew in circles around the metal-chained maypole, ran in games of tag on a playground dusted with dirt. But at home she had grown tense and vigilant, keeping alert, watching doorknobs, listening for the pad of feet down the hall, in the night, while her mama slept. She had to be aware, stay keen to the barometric changes in the atmosphere of the little house, because she knew that darkness held the thick, syrupy smell of whiskey riding warm breaths across the slurred dreams of a girl now eight years old—when her only father would stand beside her bed and put her small palm to the thing that lived there beneath the hairy curve of his belly.

She would try to shove pictures into the grainy dark, try not to see him, not feel the mash of her tiny hand into his, but she could not pretend his looming form away or conjure anything that would color the dim shadows of her bedroom, not while she looked into the dark. So she shut her eyes tight, so tight it hurt, sending bursts of light against her clenched lids. And all the while, as he moved her palm along the creature he coaxed with his own, she would see nothing but the black-eyed Susans growing along the highway, or yellow buttercups at Easter, or her mother's azalea bushes, hot pink and white against green. She would bathe herself in floral colors, fending off the dark and the molding of her fingers to the creature taking shape there, boozy breaths—all laced with the harsh, hot scent of the Camels he smoked—bearing down on her small body. She strung the flowers into garlands spiraling out around the little bed until his breaths hit hard and the thing spat venom across the pistils and velvet petals she had laced through the thick layers of the night.

When she was nine, ten, eleven, he would take her on long rides in the game preserve, slits in the rough-trunked horizon strobing sunlight into the periphery of her vision, where he lived, on the edge of a look, a quick cut of an eye, never full-on and vulnerable, never a challenging stare. She would lean her chin on her hand and hang her arm out the open window, trying to catch and hold the air, pushing her palm against the gale. Just the two of them, away from the house, furtive, like lovers trysting and traveling across the borders of contexts and closed-off emotions. He would find hidden, high-walled creek banks, where he would fire his pistol at the empty beer cans that forever clattered across the bed of his pickup. He taught her how to shoot, wrapped her small fingers around the butt of the Ruger and helped her support the weight of it, showed her how to hold it, palm cupping wrist, breathe in, let out slowly, and as shoulders drop, squeeze—no, no, squeeze, real slow, Baby Doll. That's it, that's it.

The noise of it, set off from her own thin fingers, crashed booming into the wild silence of the forest, an ear-ringing power of more dimension than she could have ever imagined, and its echo cracked and cracked its fade into a silence. And she liked it. So she practiced, asked him to teach her how to load, clean and care for the thing, squealed with the thrill of firing it, exhilarated by its deafening blasts, those sounds that had more than once chased her from her little bed. She made secret dares, vows to herself to get better, be the best, know it like an intimate friend, a confidante. In time she began to practice with even more determination, with the grim focus of a guerilla warrior, whenever he took her out for one of their rides down the red clay roads curling through the wooded, forested walls that hid them. She put aim at beer cans and milk cartons and squares of cardboard with bull's-eyes drawn on them. She exploded an olive green wine bottle she had found under her mother's bed, sending a spray of glass bits sparkling like emeralds scattered to the sky.

"Got him!" her stepfather grunted.

And she smiled at him, a coy one, the one she had learned to use early on, to maneuver him there in the unpopulated margins of her life. She could force an advantage, she had gradually discovered, could write a tune without words and suspend him in a dance. A lift of her chin, a pout of her lip, an inflection, a glance—she had found where the lines could be, if she wanted them there. She could change the course of a day with the bat of a lash, the turn of a wrist, the knowledge she had gathered and filed away during those solitary moments at his side. She could finally see who might really hold the cards, and where his weaknesses resided, and get the true lay of the land he had hidden for so many years without her ever suspecting. She squeezed the trigger.

"Got him!"

And she knew she had. Even at the age of eleven, twelve, and then, thirteen, she knew she had "got him," would get him, eventually, Jesus or no. She would take it upon herself, still a child but not a child—never, really, a child. She would take herself up on her secret dare and look at him directly, for once, eyes focused hard down the barrel of a gun, silver and straight, its lines looming outward from her fixed gaze like railroad tracks, parallel until she inched it down, real slow, breathing out, the squares of the sights put to the target at the end of her vision. She would get him and reclaim herself, take herself by her little girl's hand, dimpled and unscarred, to the place where her soul was hidden. And then, finally, the two of them would blend into each other, into the notes of the music, notes in chromatic half-steps and notes of modulation, staves winding around and nestling against the warm skin of the relative in Beaumont, Texas, where the thing with feathers could sit unabashed on its perch, and reach into its sweet, sweet depths, and sing.

LaPrade

The man rolled over in the dirt, a reddish-brown patch remaining on the left side of his face. Anyone could see that he had been crying, and he brought his fists up to rub the tears away, just as a child might. He made no move to untie the rope around his neck.

The sun was just coming up—edging its way through the ribbon of haze separating earth from sky. The haziness played tricks on the old man, mixing the greenery of spring with the blue that was always above it—or did it surround it? The man heaved himself into a sitting position to watch the rusted Studebaker raised on concrete blocks, a monument to a past he only remembered in distorted snippets. "Charmaine?" he whispered, then looked away, recognition lost.

The night's quiet still settled over the rotting wood and tarpaper shack, but soon he would hear Missy shuffling about, doing those things he imagined other women did in the morning. Boards would creak, then she would appear at the door. She would look at him and say, "You know you done bad, LaPrade." He would nod yes. Next she would put on the faded blue-and-red plaid dress that hung on the door-knob every night, walk over to the car, squat down beside it, and pee, holding onto the door handle to keep her balance. Finally she would come and untie the rope around his neck. He would promise to do better.

Missy was a lightly freckled mixture of child and woman, almost pretty when the light filtered just so. That same light, strained through a honey jar, melded the color of her eyes—an eerie echo of amber. Although her hair was brown, the light sometimes found a reddish tint, and the thick waves that spread out from a ponytail hanging down her back turned auburn at sunset.

She watched silently as LaPrade pulled some radishes for breakfast. She wore the green plastic bandeau he had bought for her at the dollar store in Isabella. It had a flower design cut into it. That made it extra-special. Over the last couple of years LaPrade had bought her more things than ever—a pop bead necklace and bracelet kit, some Romantique perfume, a ballerina pin (that was her favorite), comic books—"Archie," "Heart Throbs," "Richie Rich," and lots more. Every Saturday he walked the twelve miles into the little valley community of Isabella, bringing back some small treasure to occupy her for a while. Still, she knew that one swoop of his eyelid could reveal a soul unredeemed and threatening.

Missy didn't go into town with him often—people stared so—but once in a while she would go with him to the picture show, or the Farmer's Exchange, or to a drawing at the Sheriff's Office. Now that the child had come, trips to town were rare. The welfare check had to go less for Dollar Store perfume and more for baby things. Missy slid the green-flowered headband off, then on again, combing a few loose strands of hair back with its plastic teeth. "You know why I done it, don't you, LaPrade?"

The man straightened up, folds of flesh on his otherwise gaunt body jiggling violently with every movement, even though his movements were slow and deliberate, as was his speech. "It makes me sad when you tie me out like that, Missy." LaPrade put the radishes in a metal pail and carried it towards the car.

The woman looked at him sharply, but hints of tears threatened to reveal themselves. "You was pinching the baby. I seen you do it. That ain't right. And the rope's your doing, too. Always has been."

LaPrade set the pail on the ground by the old car, sat down in a splintery, straw-bottomed chair, and began to lick the dirt off the radishes, spitting and scraping in the cracks with his fingernails. Finally he spoke. "I b'lieve you care more for that young'un than you do for me." The tears came again, just as they had the day before, the soul he was wearing helplessly dazed.

Missy put her arms around him, holding his face close to her chest. "I do so care for you," she said. "And you ought to care for that young'un, but I got to punish you if you do it harm. I just got to." She loved LaPrade. She knew how to read him and how to tend to him, and he had needed tending ever since her mother died three years earlier—ran the car into the creek and killed herself. LaPrade had borrowed a truck and pulled the wreck out of the water, but he never found a body, and he hadn't been the same since. Missy loved him instinctively, the same way she loved her six-month-old child. She took care of them both. Yet her instincts were beginning to addle. At first she was sure that LaPrade would get over his jealousy of the baby, but the jealousy was fading into hatred now, and Missy was afraid—especially when she thought of how her father used to be.

"I ain't bad," the man sobbed.

"No, you're good, real good." Missy stroked his bald head, unconsciously avoiding the newborn soft spot.

The man turned, studied the car with smoke-gray eyes and a confused grimace, then reached out and ran his hand over the hood. Some rust stuck to his wet palm. He slowly brought the palm to his mouth and began to lick the rust, to make his hand clean, but he stopped abruptly with Missy's "I got to go see about the young'un." The man's sixty-year-old eyes followed the sway of the girl's hips, shrouded in red-and-blue plaid. His cracked lips settled into a childlike pout.

When she returned, the baby was at her breast. "LaPrade? You know tomorrow's Easter Sunday?" Missy was smiling. She always looked forward to Easter, when LaPrade would wake up before dawn to hide eggs. Exactly two hours later she would follow, dressed in her prettiest Dollar Store things, and begin to hunt. They would play hide-the-egg for days after, until the smell of rotten eggs, whose hiding places LaPrade had forgotten, filled the house and yard.

The wrinkles on the man's face rearranged themselves, settling around the sparsely toothed smile. "What do you want me to get you for Easter, Missy? I'm going into Isabella today."

"Get some of them plastic eggs—them kind that don't

go rotten," Missy said. "I seen them at the Dollar Store. They're all colors. And you can take them apart and put other surprises in them. And we can play hide-the-egg all the time 'cause they won't go rotten!"

"What color eggs you want?"

"Green," Missy said. "And pink, too. I'm going to wear my pink pop beads and my pink socks tomorrow, so get pink!"

LaPrade stood up, stretched, then began to unsnap his overalls. "Missy, do you reckon we can do business now? Hit's been a spell." And his eyes showed her the shadow of malevolence that lived behind them if she refused.

The woman nodded yes, put the baby in a cardboard box next to the car, and lay on the ground. It wouldn't take long. No. Not long at all. It never did.

✳

The red clay road wove its way down the side of the mountain for five miles before it turned into pavement. Missy always said that the county road to Isabella was ugly—no good scenery to look at—but LaPrade loved it. So skinny and gray without any of those white lines down the middle to bother a person's eyes. The way the trees coiled themselves over the strip of concrete gave him a sense of being sheltered from the rest of the world. It was rare that a car passed, and even less often that anyone offered him a ride, but he didn't mind. He didn't feel at ease with people—not even the few kin he had scattered across the county. Only Missy gave him comfort now. He loved his daughter. She takes care of me, he thought, watching with fascination as a small brown rabbit shot across the road, disappearing in the dark mass of trees and dank earth. "Yep, she shore does that. Takes real good care of me," he said aloud.

Green scents, black-eyed Susans along the edge of the road, and a feeling of Easter crept into LaPrade. Going to be a good walk, he told himself, just as he heard the soft sputtering of an engine from the hills to his back. Panic, as the old body jerked, trying to move in several directions at once; knees hitting hard on the pavement as he fell. LaPrade wanted to hide—run deep into the trees like that rabbit and hide. If only he could get far enough from the road before—but the black pickup was already in sight, beginning to slow down. Dammit, he thought, rising awkwardly. Don't want no ride.

"How you doing there, LaPrade? Want a lift?"

LaPrade grimaced pathetically, rubbing nervous palms over worn denim thighs. "Well, McCall, I just—"

"Oh, come on," the voice from the truck interrupted. "Hop in. No sense in you walking the whole way." McCall slapped the seat on the passenger's side.

The two men rode in silence for a long time, LaPrade staring down at his own hands, strong hands in spite of age, resting on his thighs. He would hurt McCall if he had to, if the man got too much into LaPrade's business. A car passed, heading in the opposite direction.

"Welfare lady," McCall noted, craning his neck to watch the blue convertible in the rear-view mirror. "Going to your place, you reckon?"

No answer. Missy will take care of it, LaPrade thought. She always did. Smart as a whip, that girl.

More silence; but finally McCall cleared his throat. "So tell me there, LaPrade—how's everything at your place?"

LaPrade's hand jerked. "Fine," he mumbled, without

looking up.

"And your girl Missy?"

"Fine. Missy's just—well—" He rubbed his hands together. "Missy's just fine," he blurted.

Silence, except for the sputtering truck, as green scents and sunshine blew steadily through the window against LaPrade's face, black-eyed Susans blurring along the roadside. McCall again cleared his throat. "To tell you the truth, LaPrade, I was hoping to catch you today. There's something—well, I figure we're neighbors and all, even if we don't live close by and don't talk much."

LaPrade could hear the blood pumping through his ears like a clock ticking frantically, low and loud.

"Is it so that Missy's done had her a baby? There's been talk of it."

LaPrade stiffened. There it was. The baby. He tried not to give McCall any sign of the hate—the intense hatred he felt for the child. Maybe if it weren't an arm baby it would be different, but the child wouldn't be ready for the ground for a long while. He could not stand to see Missy give her touch and time to anyone other than himself, but he did not dare change expression or McCall might suspect. We're kin, LaPrade told himself. We got our way of doing things. Why does anybody have to bother it? All because of that damn baby.

"All right," McCall sighed. "I just wanted you to know that there's talk. And there's going to be people looking into some things. Thought you ought to know. Is this okay?" he asked, stopping his truck in front of Stoner's Hardware Store.

LaPrade was startled by the heaviness of his body as he got out of the truck. He looked at his interrogator for the first time, mumbling a thank-you, and began his attempt to blend into the little town of Isabella, Georgia. He didn't see McCall staring after him, puzzling over such a crazy old man.

LaPrade chuckled at his reflection in the window of Stoner's Hardware. I'm going to do real good today. I been bad. I know it. But tomorrow's hide-the-egg. Out of the corner of his eye, the man could see a young woman walking beside and a little behind him. She was pretty, he suspected, because she wore a pink dress—Missy's favorite color—and she had red hair. LaPrade stopped walking as recognition came for the second time that day. Charmaine's hair had been red. Is it you? I done it. Done drove you away. You come back, you hear? Ain't going to do it no more. Ain't going to hurt you no more.

The roar of a cattle truck startled LaPrade, reminding him where he was. He could feel the perspiration on his forehead and the stares of passing people. He drew in his breath. Charmaine didn't enter his mind very often anymore, and he surprised himself when he did think of her.

The Dollar Store loomed before him. The words "Clary's Five & Dime" were still stenciled across plate-glass windows, although five-and-dimes were obsolete. Even the familiar smells hung over the store like the past it represented— month-old popcorn, stale chocolate and coconut, plastic things. The occasional ring of the antique cash register. The whir of the drawer shooting out. The wooden floor creaked as LaPrade made his way to the back left-hand corner where the toys were. Polka-dot balls, Yo-Yos, and hideously grinning dolls cluttered the glass shelves. Dolls. Baby dolls. Babies. Their plastic eyes laughed down at him, and he glared back uneasily.

"Can I help you?" An elderly saleslady was beside him,

smiling. LaPrade jerked his shoulders, standing with all his weight on his right leg.

"Yes'm. I want to buy some Easter eggs."

"Easter eggs."

He cleared his throat. "Yes'm. Them kind that don't go rotten?"

"I don't think I understand." The woman's smile suddenly became artificial.

LaPrade shifted his weight to his left leg, nervously.

"Them kind you can put other surprises in. Them—"

"Oh." The woman relaxed, her smile natural again. "Straight back and to the right." She pointed to a large Easter display.

LaPrade stared at the pyramid of stuffed rabbits, yellow-and-blue baskets full of shiny artificial grass, marshmallow chicks, and candy—every kind of candy—and cardboard fans proclaiming, "He Is Risen!" LaPrade wished that he could take it all to Missy—make her forget about the baby.

He picked up some of the plastic eggs. Twenty cents apiece. He could get two green ones, two pink ones, and still have enough left for a chocolate rabbit—a little one. Missy'd be happy with that surprise especially.

Once outside again, the sun was bright, reflecting off the pavement in glittering patterns. LaPrade squinted. He felt very proud carrying the big green bag with "Bill's Dollar Store" printed across it. He couldn't resist peeking inside the bag several times during his walk home. The chocolate bunny stared back at him from deep within the green paper prison, through the cellophane cage, with eerily accusing orange candy eyes. It startled LaPrade, but knowing what a treasure he had was also comforting.

✳

Missy had heard the automobile approaching long before it arrived. Now she and Mrs. Owens sat in the front seat. It was a convertible, looking brand-new. Missy loved the feeling of sitting in such a fancy car—even if it wasn't going anywhere.

"That sure is a pretty dress you got on, Miz Owens."

The middle-aged woman smiled. "Well, thank you, Missy. Now if we can—"

"And that perfume smells real nice, too. LaPrade buys me perfume sometimes. I got some Romantique and—"

"Now Missy, stop all this." The woman leaned forward. "You know I didn't come here to chitchat about clothes and perfume and nonsense."

"Well, that's what ladies talk about, ain't it?" Missy whined.

"Stop it now. You're trying to keep us off the subject. Now behave." She paused, lighting a cigarette. Then, in a gentler tone, "I'd like to see your baby. Where is it? May I look?"

"No?" It was a half question. Mrs. Owens touched Missy's shoulder.

"Oh, Missy, honey, did it die?"

"No'm."

"You've got to show me sooner or later. You can get aid, you know."

"My baby don't need nothing from nobody."

"Is it a boy or a girl? And is it healthy? You know, childbirth is not without hazard if you do it alone, especially at your age. And if this is your father's child, there could be serious—"

"It ain't LaPrade's," was the calm reply, but the green-flow-

54

ered bandeau was coming off and going on again nervously. "Can't you mind your own business, please, Miz Owens?"

"Missy, you are my business. And I know you aren't stupid—you could better yourself. The most important thing is for you to be honest with me."

"Yes'm."

The older woman took a deep breath. "Now, I must ask you this question again. I'm just as tired of it as you are. But please. Please answer it honestly this time. All right?"

"Yes'm."

"Has your father ever raped you?"

"No!" The tiny voice began to rise. "He ain't never done that! And I told you—it ain't his child!"

"Missy, you never cease to amaze me." Mrs. Owens calmly exhaled cigarette smoke through her nose, a menacing dragon with dyed hair. Her tone was harsh. "Now listen to me. I may be fairly new on your case, but I've learned quite a bit, so don't think you can fool me. I know you have not socialized with anyone or attended school for years. I also know you've got good sense. I just don't understand why you pretend otherwise. Could it be all these years of playing along with your father?"

Missy said nothing.

"Why did you quit going to school when your mother left? You were such a good student. Did he make you? Did he beat you? I certainly don't doubt that he beat your mother quite frequently."

"Miz Owens, Brother Claud told you them things, but he don't know. I swear he don't. We quit the Church a long time ago."

"You'd like to go back to the Church, wouldn't you?"

"Yes. I mean—no! They talk about me and LaPrade. I hate Brother Claud." But guilt was there. Missy began to cry.

Mrs. Owens touched Missy's shoulder. "It's not your fault. Don't you see he's always been a disturbed man? And he's getting old before his years, Missy. Feeble-minded. But we can fix that. Now, he's never done you any good. There are lots of agencies that we could—"

"You leave! Right now!" The bandeau was moving on and off more rapidly as Missy sobbed. "Why can't you people just leave us alone? We do just fine." She curled up in a ball next to the car door. This was different. Mrs. Owens had never before been so determined to make her change everything.

The woman lit another cigarette. She pulled Missy close to her. "Honey"—her voice became softer again—"honey, if you're doing just fine here, then why are you so upset?"

"You can't have my baby," Missy hiccupped. "And you can't—well, you can't take LaPrade and send him away from me nowhere."

"Don't you worry about that yet, honey. But do you worry about how he might mistreat the child?" She rested her head on the steering wheel for a moment, then raised it, looking, Missy thought, very sad. "Let me tell you one more thing, Missy." There was a small silence, then, "We think your mother is alive. It's not certain, of course, but she may be in Atlanta, using the name Charlotte Spurlynne. Here. I've written it down for you. Now why would your mother want to run away, do you think?"

Missy wondered briefly why she wasn't surprised, and spoke without emotion. "Well, she always liked Atlanta. And she was pretty. Real pretty. Lots of boys liked her, but there weren't nothing to it."

"Your daddy didn't like that, did he? Especially since he was so much older than your mother. It made him mad, didn't it?"

"Sometimes. Sometimes he was mean to her, and sometimes she was mean. Sometimes LaPrade called her bad things. But she was a good Christian. Brother Claud said so at the memorial service. LaPrade ain't mean no more," she lied.

"How was he mean? Did he beat her?"

"I don't remember," Missy answered quickly, her voice rising. "Can't you just leave us be? He ain't mean!" she yelled, slamming her way out of the car.

Mrs. Owens threw the burning remains of her cigarette on the ground. "All right," she said calmly, shaking her head. "I'm leaving—for now, anyway. I think we've actually made progress today, but, Missy, if you just think about that baby of yours. Think about your mother. There's a lot we can do for all of you. Think about that, all right?"

The blue convertible soon disappeared down the red clay road. It didn't even take much time for the cloud of dust left behind to disintegrate. Missy stood and watched the burning cigarette until the fire reached the filter and it gradually went out. Then she went into the house to tend to her child.

It wasn't the house she had grown up in with Charmaine. That house was further up above the creek. There had been a kitchen table, some nice furniture, and pictures of Jesus on the walls. LaPrade boarded it up after Charmaine was gone and forbade Missy to set foot in it again even though he visited it every once in a while. She had not allowed herself to miss it much until now.

Their present home was an abandoned shack with a sparse kitchen, a crude shower, and a shithouse down a trail near the creek. But it was enough for LaPrade. She knew to go along with him over the years, keep him from turning on her. Be a good daughter. But I am fifteen now—like Mama when I was born. And now I am a mama, too. Missy sat in the doorway of the shack, the baby at her breast. She could see LaPrade walking toward her about half a mile down the road. "Yonder he comes, baby. Bringing Easter eggs. You like that?"

The child replied with passive sucking noises. "He's a good man," she said, then whispered, "oh, I know he's bad from time to time—like pinching you. He just needs to be took care of." She reached up, touched her bandeau, and thought about how nice LaPrade was to buy her pretty things. She didn't like to punish him. It wasn't any easier now than it had been the first time—the day after he had given up the search for her mother's body. She had been twelve then, confused by the man her father was becoming and the strange changes in her parents over the years. But he had begged her. "I thought some lies about Charmaine," he had whined, like a little boy. "I'm bad. You got to purnish me, Missy."

She had been frightened. He had always done the punishing, the beating, and the deciding of everything. But he was handing her a rope, begging to be punished for his wife's death. At first Missy had thought he wanted to be hanged, but she couldn't do it and he didn't have enough left within him to do it himself. Terrified, she had solved the problem only by using the first thing she noticed—an old, but sturdy, fence post. One end of the rope around the post, the other around her father's neck. Missy's night, alone in the house, was filled with intermittent sounds of LaPrade's guilt, occasional thuds, and cries of pain as he ran out the length of the rope and was thrown to the ground.

"Charmaine, you can't be dead!" he would scream. "You come back here! I ain't going to say no more! Nothing about Fred Culver or Adon McCall or none of the others! I ain't! I swear to God I ain't!" Those words had become more jumbled as the night moved into dawn. Finally she had crept out of the house and held him next to her—pitied him—done business with him. It was her obligation. She was kin. She accepted it. It was a sacrifice—a Christian sacrifice; any guilt that crept in she learned to dissolve. It was a matter of survival. These days she was coming to see that her own child must also survive.

"Baby, you sure are pretty." Missy spoke aloud again. "Just like my ballerina pin. Sort of hard to tell you two apart."

The screen door squenched loudly, slamming behind her father. "Wait'll you see!" LaPrade cried, laughing. "Wait'll you see!" he sang over and over, dangling the sack in front of Missy's excited face, dancing around in crazy circles.

"Give it, give it!" she squealed, laying the baby on the floor, chasing LaPrade outside and the fifty yards to the creek, where he collapsed in the weeds, hugging the bag to his chest.

"You know you cain't see till tomorrow."

"Well, I reckon I will see tomorrow." Missy was too out of breath to play any longer.

"You take care of that Welfare lady today?"

"Told her to let us be," she answered, wondering if she should try to share her thoughts with him. No, she decided, I ain't going to spoil no Easter Sunday. I can let him have that, can't I?

"I thought about Charmaine today," LaPrade said. "There was a red-haired woman looked just like her in Isabella." He scratched his elbow. "Missy? What you reckon made me call her all them names? She didn't—"

Missy looked at him sharply. "Now don't you go feeling bad, and don't you go crying. Tomorrow's hide-the-egg."

He nodded and gazed blankly at the creek, mumbling, looking helpless the way he did from time to time. So different from the angry, accusing father of her childhood, who drew blood and defiance from her mother as Missy huddled in corners praying for God to make him stop. Missy shivered as a phantom rabbit scooted across her grave, reminding her not to think forbidden thoughts. She was beginning to get to know her mother much better.

"Come on, LaPrade." Missy took his hand and led him back to the house; she would cheer him up. They would giggle and tease one another, plan for hours about Easter. Then she noticed the baby on the floor, felt the uneasiness again, and ran to comfort it.

✳

A good day for hide-the-egg, LaPrade thought as he crept out of the little house, careful not to disturb Missy. Outside, the mist took on a yellowish cast from sunshine soaking through green leaves. Fresh dew on clumps of grass made it look like the artificial Easter kind at the dollar store. Pretty, he told himself, reaching for the eggs in the big green bag. Missy'll be so happy.

The man gently carried the two pink eggs over to the old automobile. It would be a perfect hiding place. Giggling like a little boy with a secret, he put the first egg behind one of the concrete blocks supporting the vehicle. The second went under the front seat. "She'll never find that one," he chuckled aloud, the loose flesh on his neck nodding in agreement. A green egg was situated in a clump of grass by the house. The man praised himself for being so smart about mixing the colors. LaPrade stood still for a long time, thoughtfully searching out a hiding place for the last egg. As his eyes rested on one of the peeling pieces of tarpaper, he smiled. I done good, he told himself as he wedged the egg behind the flap of paper. A few termites emerged from holes in the wood.

"You just can't figure out what that big old green thing is, can you?" LaPrade said to the frantic insects. "Well, this is the best hiding place ever, so don't you go messing with it." He laughed at himself. "Talking to bugs," he muttered.

Now it was time for the real treasure. Slowly, ceremoniously, the old man took the chocolate rabbit out of the cellophane. He set the candy animal in the radish patch, proud of himself for being so smart about it. The orange eyes seemed to follow him as he went back into the house.

She'll be awake soon, he thought, almost tripping over the baby. The child gazed up at him blankly, not making a sound. LaPrade had a sudden urge to crush it—place his foot on the child's tiny body until all life was gone. No, he told himself firmly, that would be bad, and Missy likes it. Likes to play with it. Suddenly, LaPrade had a wonderful idea. I'll hide the baby. He began to get more excited. Missy's gon' love this game. He clumsily lifted the child, stiff arms held out from his old body. It still didn't make a sound—but then, it hardly ever cried.

By the time he returned, the woman was standing in the doorway—all blue-and-red plaid and pink.

"I never seen you looking so pretty, Missy."

"You think so? You think my pop beads look good? I was going to mix some blue in with them, but pink's such a pretty color all by itself." She looked at him expectantly.

"It's fine, Missy. You're prettier'n ever."

"LaPrade?" Missy walked toward him and touched his elbow. "Where's the baby? I couldn't find it when I waked up." She must not show anger, must not confuse him or rile him. She knew the danger in that.

The man smiled. "Don't you worry. I done moved it. Right now you got to hunt the eggs!" he exclaimed.

The woman hesitated, then giggled, knowing that she must, and immediately ran toward the car. "You always hide one here, fool." Laughter. Green and yellow sunshine. It went by much too quickly to suit LaPrade. He was disappointed when, after the last egg was found, Missy again asked about the baby.

"Missy, I can't tell. You got to find it—like the eggs. It'll be fun!" But Missy wasn't smiling. That wasn't supposed to happen. She was supposed to be pleased.

"You better not have hurt it, LaPrade," she said evenly.

"Missy, now don't be mad. It's a game. It's—" He stopped, afraid of the way she was looking at him.

"You tell me where it is. Right now, you hear me?"

The man slowly turned his face toward the car, then the creek, then back to Missy. He began to cry.

"I done forgot," he sobbed.

The woman froze, not believing. "No," she whispered, then screamed, "What did you do to it?"

LaPrade looked thoughtful. "Don't worry, Missy. She ain't dead. I seen her in Isabella yesterday, remember?"

But his daughter wasn't listening. She was running—running hard, pushing through morning-moist green leaves, head jerking frantically left to right, searching. Where you at, baby? You under that old car? LaPrade, he ain't right, Mama, but you lied and I need my young'un. Missy was breathless, sobbing, running from car to house to clumps of trees and back again. There was not enough of her to get to all the places the baby might be.

She lifted the hinged door set in the floor of the shack where LaPrade stored potatoes and moonshine. But at once she realized she had already looked here, her panic pushing her into a randomly repetitious search of only the most obvious places: the shithouse, the old car trunk, a kudzu-covered aluminum boat, the washtub where she had bathed her doll babies only a few months before.

Frantic phrases throbbed through her brain. *Baby ain't no doll. Baby's real. Ain't no plastic toy. Baby can die. LaPrade killed it? No, please. Need my young'un. Got to be it. You done made a choice, Mama. Mama.*

Suddenly Missy knew. She began to run the fifty yards towards the creek, the word *mama, mama, mama* drumming through her head, setting a cadence for her breathing.

She saw it as she approached the water. A tiny, mud-caked child, making strange little choking sounds. "Oh, baby," she whispered, gently picking it up. "Baby, poor baby," she cooed over and over, softly, as she walked toward the house. Mizres Owens must be right. It must be so. As Missy wiped the mud from her baby's face, she knew.

LaPrade was exactly where she had left him, only he was sitting now, rocking back and forth, crying, "My fault, my fault."

"You could've kilt it!" Missy said sharply.

"Oh, Missy, I ain't—"

"You could've kilt it! Just like—well, just like you could've kilt Mama."

"But she ain't dead," LaPrade said. "I seen her in Isabella."

Missy sighed. "You just ain't right, LaPrade. Now you know what I got to do?"

The man obediently walked over to the old fence post and allowed Missy to tie the rope around his neck. She sat in the doorway of the shack and stared at her father for a long time, glancing occasionally at the rusty automobile. She held her child close, reaching up every now and then to comb loose strands of hair back with the plastic headband. "You know what we got to do, baby?" she whispered. The child merely gazed up at her, some dark mud still caked around its neck and face. The woman sighed, stood up, and went to LaPrade. She gently kissed the top of his baldhead. "Goodbye, Daddy." She stroked his cheek. "I got to do it. I just got to." But she walked uncertainly down the dirt road away from the shack.

"Where you going, Missy?"

She stopped. Turned around. "Leaving." Tears were finally allowed to touch the faint freckles on her cheeks.

"You cain't!" LaPrade screamed. "Where you going?"

"Don't know," she sobbed. "To see Miz Owens. Maybe to Atlanta."

"You don't know what you're doing!" The man called out. "Look here, Missy. Look here what I got you. In the radish patch. Look here. A candy rabbit!"

She hesitated, then continued walking. "Done made my mind up, baby. Ain't no candy rabbit going to change it," she mumbled.

"Missy!" he yelled, running out the length of the rope, feet rushing from under him, falling hard on his back against the dirt. "I ain't going do it no more!" he yelled louder, pounding his fists in the dirt. "I promise! You don't care nothing about that young'un. It ain't even got no name! Missy!"

The woman stopped abruptly. After standing very still for a full minute, shoulders rising, falling, rising, she turned one last time and screamed, "William! Its name's William!"

The man lay in the dirt. She was out of sight now. Had been for quite a while. LaPrade's gray-filmed eyes gazed blankly at the chocolate rabbit. It was beginning to melt, and the orange eyes were sliding down the dark-brown cheeks. By mid-afternoon it was covered with ants and flies and even a few yellow jackets.

From *In the Dark of the Moon*

Royce Fitzhugh was feeling pretty good for a change, knowing there would be a way out soon, away from Sumner, Georgia, away from his slut of a mother, and out into the world, a world that was lining up for war, he hoped. The only sad thing about leaving was that he wouldn't see Elizabeth Lacey, who was finally, at twelve, coming into her own, in exactly the way he predicted to her at a political rally, a little over two years earlier.

Royce had always been curious about Elizabeth, ever since the days when she visited Chen Ling and the three of them would toss horseshoes in the Chinaman's backyard or play dominoes on the porch. But now Royce was seventeen years old, a frustrated pursuer of girls, still watching Elizabeth, ever and always miles ahead of the other girls her own age, but never more than now. What he saw in Elizabeth these days promised to overtake even the girls his age, girls already three, four, five years older than she, girls who criticized her while they vied for her attention, hoping some of the mystique might rub off on them. These days, when Elizabeth visited the Chinaman, Chen Ling blushed and looked down with increasing frequency. These days, Royce felt a shift in the repartee—both spoken and unspoken—between himself and Elizabeth. These days, boys in the upper grades were mentioning her name, looking at Royce with a new respect, keenly aware of his access to her. Royce knew what she promised to represent for the boys in town: the magnetic force in their tiny universe, the sun at the center of their solar system, already exemplified by their willingness to take up one, just one, of Lizzie's dares, win her delight when, the task complete, she charged over to offer a hug, a kiss, or, for himself, Royce hoped, someday, that confection of a galaxy between her legs.

At only twelve years of age Elizabeth was getting noticed.

But Royce also knew that Elizabeth had something much more than extraordinary good looks, something not as obvious as overly developed curves and thick, wavy hair and sapphire blue eyes; but something subtle and stinging and sensual, some kind of musky certainty that promised to intimidate as it beckoned, overlaid with the ripening glaze of potential, just on the verge, poised there, on the sweet verge of something he sensed in the most primal way. Hell, she was just a kid, on paper; but he could always see that those blue eyes knew things, that she was watching far into some peripheral kind of anticipation and had the carnal capacity to wash over men with the pull of a rip current, carrying them out to sea on a sweet, rough-and-tumble tide. It was the precursor of swollen flesh and hidden renderings of sexuality, the burst of an egg through a Fallopian bloom, the sigh of a scent of that first heat, folds of skin pushed out, making ready, waiting for the lunar signal to set it all in motion.

"You've been bruised, on the inside, like me," Elizabeth said to him from time to time.

"Why do you think that?"

"I've seen it in your mama's eyes," she'd say, and her own eyes would fill with tears, but only for a second.

Bruised on the inside? It seemed to make her feel tender and kindly toward him, so he let her believe it was true. Hell, he would let her believe anything as long as it gave him an edge, a shot at being the one who would get close, who would conquer that sweet, rich part of her. If she wanted him to be bruised, by god, she could have him that way, though he was anything but bruised.

Royce had, in fact, calloused over so many times he was hard as stone by the time he was twelve. His daddy was long gone, had spent only five years as a fixture in Royce's life, a presence that reminded him daily how worthless and stupid he was, welting Royce's back with a razor strop or a buggy whip, wrenching his little arm in its socket in order to lay into his bare buttocks with one of his brogans, snatched in anger from beneath the sofa. Royce hated him, resented his mother's silence, her tacit approval of Lucas Fitzhugh's brand of discipline. The only days his daddy missed out on administering a beating were those welcome periods when he disappeared for weeks at a time, on a drinking and cheating tear, his mama said, seeming relieved that her husband was at the moment not a presence in her life, a relief that gave way to fear and fretting over money, which gave way to nights out, away from Royce, when she stayed out late, sometimes overnight. Royce had vague memories of playing in his crib in the dark, in the silence, having cried himself spent, and without anyone coming to see to him.

The Chinaman came, though, from next door, every so often, when he heard Royce screaming for a mama who was not there. On those nights Chen Ling would sit by his crib and tell stories half in English, half in Chinese, until Royce fell asleep. By the time he was three, Royce knew not to mention Chen Ling's presence in their home—his mother had gone next door one Sunday and railed at Ling for meddling, screaming and cussing so loud the law had to come—and by the time Royce was four, he began to notice that his mama had grocery money on those mornings after she had stayed out all night.

His daddy would finally come home and there would be cursing accusations and arguments and his mother thrown into walls or slapped around or punched. "You need to sport a shiner for a while behind that shit," Lucas sometimes said. Then he proceeded to give her one while Royce looked on, at once both afraid for her and glad she was getting what she allowed Royce to get with brutal regularity.

Finally, one day when Royce was five years old, perhaps after weighing the solitary freedom Lucas's absences afforded her against the misery and cruelty he brought, his mama finally stood up for her son. His daddy had just cussed him and slid the belt out of his pants, whipping through the loops, a quick leather snake to accompany the venom of his words: "You goddamn idiot. Why you want to be such a goddamn idiot, boy?"

But on this day his mama stepped forward with a Colt .45, a gift from one of her man friends, leveled at Lucas Fitzhugh, a gesture that said, without hesitation, Stop. It was the first time Royce had ever seen that side of his mother, the reservoir of determination, the certainty that acted in this brief battle as the element of surprise.

Lucas let go of his arm as an expression of shock took his face. "Woman, have you gone around the bend?"

"You ain't going to do him that way," she said. "It will come to your fists by the time he's eight, and then what? Either you'll kill him or he'll get growed up and kill you. Best for you to get on gone, right now, before I kill you instead."

Royce always thought it strange how quickly his daddy left, and how permanently, too. Royce never laid eyes on him again, and if his mama did, well, she never let on. His daddy didn't even pack up his clothes. Lucas Fitzhugh offered up no argument, no inclination to compromise, just a sneer of a snarl at Royce's mama, with the words, "He ain't none of mine noway."

The boy watched him walk away, the back of his neck wearing the V of dark hair that curled all the way down his back, beneath the work shirt, arms bowed out at his sides, fists balled up, itching for a fight. It was only a few months later that the implications of his daddy's last words began to sink in, when his ears picked up on the whispers of the decent folks of the town, how Mona Anne Fitzhugh was a two-dollar whore for sale down by the tracks, down near nigger town. And, even though Royce could not fully comprehend—not yet—what a "two-dollar whore" was, he could not help but notice that, once Lucas was gone for good, the men began to trickle in to the little shack, for drinks and laughter, until his mother's bedroom door swung shut and the bedsprings squawked out a rhythm picking up faster and faster. Sometimes the boy heard mumbled curses or loud moans, even shouts that startled him out of his slumber and into those provinces of the man-woman world he was only beginning to fathom, and much too early.

When he was six, seven, eight, he wandered out on the back porch when the bedsprings started screeching. He lay on the glider and waited for trains to roar past and drown out the sounds. Sometimes the Chinaman stepped out on his own porch, saw the boy lying there, and whispered, "Come here, Roy Fitz. Come play domino Chen." And they would steal into the Chinaman's little shotgun house and play rounds of dominoes until Royce was sleepy enough to go home and crawl into bed.

"You stay night if want," the Chinaman always said.

But Royce never stayed. He asked his mother, once, if he could stay overnight with the Chinaman, but she squashed the idea fast. "Hell no, you can't sleep over there with that slanty-eyed devil. He ain't like us," she said. "He's a foreigner. They got strange ways that you ain't liable to know what he might be up to. Worser than a nigger. Now go on and don't ask me about that Chinaman again."

So Royce continued, when he was eight, nine, to sleep on the glider some nights, play dominoes at the Chinaman's house other nights, and feel relief on the nights when his mama did not have company. It was the late nights that got him, though, when he heard a knock at the door around midnight, the swish of his mama's bare feet against linoleum, a hushed, murmured conversation ending with his mama's, "Okay. Come on in." Then muted words from the front room, the room next to his, followed by his mother's moans and the uneven squeak of the bedsprings, the sound that drove into him like a jackhammer, stirred in him the suspicion that his mama could not be okay, not with that racket going on, yet the human sounds he heard seemed to be expressions of pleasure. It did not make sense, and so finally, at ten, Royce slipped to her cracked bedroom door one late night, just past midnight, just as the mattress began to squawk. He put his face to the doorway's opening and let his eyes adjust to the dark, making out a man's bare backside, that bare backside moving toward and away from the bed. And then he realized it was his mama the man was moving onto, and her knees were drawn up and he heard her say, "That's good, Daddy. Do it like that. Show me." Then the man moved faster and Royce was afraid to stay there, afraid of what he would see next that he did not understand.

He tried, in his child's way, to get the Chinaman to explain it over dominoes one night.

"Ah, no," Chen said. He seemed embarrassed and just as awkward as Royce had felt in asking, the Chinaman's English breaking up even more from the awkwardness. "No say much. Maybe say too much. Mama no make fuck. Now you play domino."

By the time he was eleven, Royce had figured out what the man was doing to his mother, there on the bed with her knees drawn up, and he had figured out some of the other things she probably did with them, things he heard older boys bragging about. And it was around the same time that some of the boys at school began to taunt him once in a while on the playground, where they played baseball to the peripheral squeals of the smaller children and thick ropes dangling tire swings groaned their deep-toned rhythms.

"Know where we can get a piece of tail, Fitzhugh?"

"A piece of tail for sale?"

"Who can pleasure many a man?" one rhyme went. "Go see moaning Mona Anne."

Royce knew he was fated to be either a sissy or a scrapper, with no in-between. He chose to be a scrapper, to be Lucas Fitzhugh's son, whether or not he was claimed as a son, and beat the shit out of anybody who teased him, and then some, serving up preemptive beatings before the other boys had the chance to think. Sometimes he lost the fight, but most times he won, getting a meaner and meaner reputation that eventually silenced those inclined to say anything about Mona Anne—to his face, anyway.

So it was that, as Royce entered adolescence, his already muted love for his mother had gown tainted with disgust, and he spent more and more time away from the shack and the men and the woman who spread her legs to keep him in milk and eggs and corn meal and shame. He never mentioned her to his friends in high school and they were by then mature enough and kind enough not to mention her, either, even though there was the occasional rumor that some of the athletes were going to go visit Mona Anne this night or that one. The bitter taste of her name in its carnal contexts slid down his throat and deep into his gut, eating away any kind of respect or caring he might have been able to conjure up for her. Finally, in the months leading up to his seventeenth year, he began to see a way out.

The Germans were all over Europe and folks claimed it wouldn't be long before Roosevelt went on and committed to helping out, running the Krauts back to Berlin, and Royce aimed to be signed up and in on that detail if it happened.

He even began to hope for it, in spite of the fact that the popular sentiment in Blackshear County was that Roosevelt had no business even thinking about sending troops. Royce didn't care whose opinion was right; he only wanted to get the hell away from his whore of a mama, away from the stares of the church folks, and maybe even come back a hero in the process. He already had a career for himself in mind. He had taken to killing time around the sheriff's office, talking tough with the High Sheriff, sometimes running errands for him and Deputy Jack, cleaning up for a tip or two. Old Man Lacey seemed to like him, telling him more than a few times, "You got a hard edge to you, Royce, and I guess you come by it honest. You ought to get into law enforcement."

"Would you take me on?"

"You just a pup. I need me a full-growed feist. Get out in the world and get some experience. Then we'll take another look."

It was during his days as a hanger-on at the sheriff's office that he began to plot an attempt to worm his way into Elizabeth's heart in earnest. She was young, certainly, but it was not uncommon for girls of twelve, thirteen, fourteen, to be married, here in the rural part of the state. Maybe he could rescue her from her burgeoning reputation as a flirt—she was, after all, coming out of her social seclusion, and dramatically, to amuse herself with the antics of a few of the boys around town—and make a war bride of her, or at least make an engagement come about.

He knew it was a long shot, though, knew she had a flip attitude about having and keeping a boyfriend, pronounced it "a bore." Moreover, she did not even seem to care that there were social codes demanding adherence or that folks looked to judge the missteps of others on an hourly basis. The gossip about Mona Anne's and his low-level social status always ate at him; Elizabeth cared not one whit about the talk she generated with her wild actions as well as her simple ones, such as strolling through town with Hotshot trailing after. Hotshot had been orphaned over to the jailhouse, certainly—and as a young boy— becoming Elizabeth's childhood playmate, but she took no note of his skillet-black skin or his simple-minded demeanor. She cast thoughts of propriety to the side, in most matters, like the day she confirmed her sexual confidence, just strolled right into the sheriff's office, where Royce sat alone doing some filing for Mr. Jack.

"Where's Josephine?" she asked, referring to one of a couple of courthouse cats that roamed in and out of the sheriff's office, the office of the judge of probate, the county clerk's office, animals who served as pets for those county employees who took the time to feed them. Long blonde braids hung down her back, brushing at her tiny waist.

"I don't know," he said, rolling his eyes as Hotshot followed her into the room. He couldn't for the life of him understand Elizabeth's willingness to put up with Hotshot's idiot ways.

"Oh, but I want to pet her," Elizabeth said.

"She's probably off somewhere getting knocked up again. I think she's about ready to be. Again. Why don't you send the nigger to find her?"

"Shut up, Royce," she said. "Hey," she said, sitting on the sill of the open window, turning sideward, propping her feet on the sill as well, "you think you'll ever get sent to go fight those Germans?"

It was an autumn afternoon. She wore a light green

shirtwaist dress, patterned with cherries, apples, and grapes across thin cotton, thin enough for Royce to know the new secrets her body was keeping, the fresh, rounded rises at her chest, unencumbered by a second dressing of an undershirt or even, he suspected, step-ins; and the juncture of her thighs, the slope of those very thighs set off by the sun spilling its light through the open window. Hell, she was just twelve years old, but she did something to him.

"If I do, you're going to see some flat-out dead Germans," Royce said, thinking how that would sure as hell give him some experience in the world to put before Campbell Lacey.

"My grandmother says they're running crazy all over Europe."

"Well, that's a fact. Crazy as hell. Done took Poland, France, coming right at England."

"My daddy said I was crazy as a one-eyed dog." This came from Hotshot, who was standing at the bulletin board, staring at "Wanted" posters.

Royce could hardly abide Hotshot, with his stupid sayings and his gappy-toothed grin. He was close to Royce in age but acted like a little kid, had been a fixture at the jailhouse for years, had become a source of amusement for the townspeople who threw him change when he sang and danced on the street.

"You aren't crazy, Hotshot," Elizabeth said. "You're original."

"Why you got to carry him around everywhere you go?" Royce chewed on a toothpick he took from Jack Lacey's desk drawer.

"I don't 'carry' him anywhere. He's my shadow. That's what my daddy says."

Royce rolled his eyes again, not believing Mr. Jack condoned his daughter running all over creation with a nigger that was probably up to no good, putting on an act for the white folks. "Well, you ought to be careful. Do you even know what people think about it and what they say?"

"Why would I care?"

"Well, because of your reputation, I reckon."

"Who am I trying to impress? The people who think they are so good and then talk bad about other people? I don't care about any of what anybody says."

"Not even about what they say he done on that train that time?"

"Shh!"

Hotshot whirled around. "I didn't, I didn't, I didn't," he said.

Elizabeth got up and took Hotshot by the arm. "It's okay, now. Stop that." She led him to a chair by the door.

"He ain't going to get that gun. Is he? I didn't," Hotshot said, eyes large and fearful, looking for the weapon associated with that specific time and place and incident.

"No gun," Elizabeth said. "Don't worry, Hotshot."

"I can get you a gun," Royce grinned. "Does your shadow want a gun?"

"Shut up, Royce," she said, and he kind of liked the way she said it, so he did.

"I didn't, I didn't, I didn't," Hotshot whimpered.

"Wait here," she said, stepping out into the hallway, turning back to Royce. "Don't get him scared any more than he is," she said, "or I'll ..."

"Or you'll what?"

"Just don't!"

"Yes, sir!" he said, saluting her, playing at being a soldier.

Royce glared at the boy sitting opposite him. Hotshot did not look up, only rubbed his palms back and forth across his thighs, staring down at the backs of his black hands.

Goddamn retard, Royce thought. One day he's going to do something crazy, hurt somebody, and then what? Those Laceys were loony as hell, letting a girl like Elizabeth—just now coming into a more inviting kind of womanhood than most, a rare kind, even—take up with a nigger who was bound to step over the line, would have to step over it, being grown, if he—and here was a thought that made the blood burn through Royce's veins: if he hadn't already.

When Elizabeth returned she was carrying Josephine, a gray and orange tabby with honey-colored eyes. "Here, Hotshot," she said, laying the cat in his lap.

Hotshot rubbed the cat's back. "Josephine's a crazy cat," he said. The animal mewed a guttural sound and writhed against Hotshot's palm.

"You really don't care what folks think about you? Royce asked.

"No, I don't," Elizabeth said. "The Bible's full of warnings about gossip and judgment."

"Still and all, you ought to know folks don't think a girl your age should be roaming the streets with a grown nigger."

"He's not grown," Elizabeth said. "My Aunt Frances says he'll never be grown in his mind. And even if he was, I would still take up time with him, even more, because he would be more like a friend and not a shadow."

"A friend?"

"Yes."

"Well you better be goddamn glad he ain't grown in

the head, then, 'cause you ain't got no business, at your age, taking up with a nigger friend."

"That's all you know," Elizabeth said, as Josephine mewed in agreement, wallowing against Hotshot's thighs.

"Yeah, I do know," he said. "You need yourself a big brother kind of guy, to look out for you." He grinned, letting his gaze glide down her body.

"I'll never need a boy to look out for me," Elizabeth said.

The cat mewed another deep-noted sound.

"Oh, yes, you will," Royce said. "Believe me. I know. You're turning into something that's going to need a lot of looking out for."

"Says who?"

"Says me. I hear things."

"Like what?"

"Like how you smoke cigarettes on the street."

"So?"

"I bet you already been into the brandy, just like your mama."

Elizabeth shrugged.

"Well, have you?" It was appealing, Royce thought, the picture of a liquored-up Elizabeth with her braids down, lying on top of him, loose hair hanging down across her face and into his.

She smiled. "Maybe."

Royce laughed. "I heard how you dared Bobby Dees to steal a pack of his daddy's Picayunes, how the preacher caught y'all smoking on the front steps of the church."

"I'll say it again." She flipped one braid back. "So?"

"And I heard you got Stew Weatherall to steal all the ladies' corsets from the Empire department store round the corner."

Elizabeth broke into laughter herself then. "We had the best time lacing them onto the pine trees by the picnic grounds!"

"Yeah, I heard old Stew got a whipping from his daddy behind that."

Elizabeth rolled her eyes. "I'm afraid so," she sighed with exaggerated drama.

"I don't reckon anybody whipped you?"

She laughed again, and the sound melted over him.

"You didn't get in no kind of trouble?"

"Well, my mama got drunk and my grandmamma fussed, but my daddy just had to laugh. It was a funny prank, that's all."

"What about your granddaddy?"

She bit her lip and her eyes shadowed over with a kind of angry sadness. "He did his usual prank with his pistol and—"

A sudden screech and the pop of a hiss came from the cat.

"Josephine, what?" Hotshot shouted.

The cat had leapt from his lap and lay writhing and growl-mewing on the floor. Then she rolled over, the front half of her body in a crouch, her hind end raised, twisting at her rib cage, making more feral sounds, long, drawn-out groans.

Hotshot stood, agitated. "What you doing, crazy cat?"

"It's all right," Elizabeth said, and Royce winced at the calming effect her words had on the solidly muscled, solidly black teenager. She got up and squatted down next to the cat, her dress sliding up over her knees. Royce wanted to be in front of her, getting a look up that thin dress.

"She's in heat again," Elizabeth said. "Remember the last batch of kittens, Hotshot? Remember I told you she had a litter once or twice a year, spring and fall?"

"She ain't hot," he said, kneeling, putting his hand on the cat's haunches. Josephine wriggled against his touch.

Royce stood, thinking how Elizabeth had not one whit of shame in her, to be squatting down watching a needing-to-be-fucked cat with a horny nigger.

"She wants a boy cat," Elizabeth said, pointing to a place beneath the cat's tail, where its fur made a deep black Y shape, "to put it in her."

"Like them dogs at Miss Martha and them's house," Hotshot said.

"Yes, like that. But cats have really vicious fights, the boys against the boys, and even the girl fights it. And when the boy cat finally gets on her, she makes all kinds of racket, like she is now."

Royce had maneuvered around to the chair in front of Elizabeth, who had dropped back on her rear, sitting with her knees drawn up now, ankles crossed, not caring, enthralled as she was with watching the cat, that her dress crept further up her thighs. Royce glanced at Hotshot, to see if he was looking up that dress, but the ungrown boy was only studying the cat's rolling, writhing motions along with Elizabeth.

"Poor thing," Elizabeth said. "She wants a boy cat really bad."

"Just what we need around here," Royce said. "Another mess of kittens for me to have to carry off and drown." He let his eyes take in the flesh of her thighs, already promising himself he would touch them one day.

"No! Don't talk about things like that! And don't you dare hurt her babies," Elizabeth said. "Ever." She scratched Josephine's head.

Royce did not tell her that it was her own grandfather who routinely gave him the order to execute the kittens no one cared to adopt from the courthouse grounds. Usually he carried them in a croaker sack to Cane Creek on the edge of town, weighted the sack down and chunked it under the bridge. Sometimes, though, he would wring their necks or pound their skulls with a heavy rock before throwing them in the water, but that was only if there weren't too many of them and he didn't need a sack to carry them all.

"Do you see how puffy it gets?" she said. "And sometimes the way they carry on is like they're really hurting."

As if in response, Josephine let howl an even longer cat moan, flipping to her back, twisting back and forth sideways against the floor. Royce let his eyes find the place, the white cotton of her step-ins, and stay there a while, wondering what she looked like, right—there, thinking it would maybe be smooth and pink and sweet, not like the overused, worn-out one that certainly resided between his mother's routinely pounded thighs. He conjured up the image of Elizabeth's flesh, where his gaze rested, shucking the undergarment from his vision, seeing it there, waiting for him. Then he noticed the silence in the room, save for the cat's fevered growls, and he glanced up. Elizabeth was watching him, a knowing smirk on her face.

Royce looked at Hotshot but the boy was focused on the cat's contortions. "You ought not to go letting your skirt up," he said.

"Do you think I give a care if you look at my under-drawers?"

"Well, you should," he said. "Look at you. You ain't even trying to cover up."

"You're pretty stupid," she said, scratching Josephine's head. "You really think I care if you see."

"You know what the Bible says about modesty, don't you?"

"How do you know what it says?" she countered.

"Because the Primitive Baptists are all the time hauling me to Sunday school, trying to make me out a lost lamb."

"Are you a lost lamb?"

He liked the way she looked at him in that moment, all concern and tenderness, so he replied, "Maybe I am," before adding, "but hadn't you better cover up your drawers?"

She smiled. "Maybe you better read more Bible verses if you're so concerned about my drawers."

"What the hell more I got to learn from the Bible?" She still had not moved, and his eyes kept making fleeting returns to the white cotton underwear.

"Well, for one thing, the Bible says, 'Flee also youthful lusts'. That's Second Timothy." And she giggled as Royce's face went red. "Let's go, Hotshot. We'll go find Josephine a boyfriend. Pull me up."

Royce watched Hotshot take her hand and bring her to her feet, hating the boy's familiarity with her, the ease with which she cared for the jailhouse orphan. He sat for a long time after they left, watching goddamned Josephine carrying on like a cathouse whore, growling and gyrating. He thought of the untouched place between Elizabeth's legs. He hoped like hell it was soft as a hen's feather, pristine, that the whispers of speculation about Hotshot and the long-ago train ride were just rumors. Was that place she had just shown him really untouched, unlike the one used so regularly by Moaning Mona Anne? Elizabeth sure acted like she knew more than other girls her age. He stared at the cat, struck again by how Elizabeth had described Josephine's estrous with such utter unselfconsciousness, just as she refused to feel embarrassed to have him studying her underwear, imagining her flesh. Shit, she would probably describe the fine details of her own body with an equal absence of shame, a thought which teased excitement into him. He put his hand to his crotch. Maybe she would do that sometime, tell him what she saw when she looked at herself.

Josephine let out a piercing wail that droned into a groan and lifted her haunches again, curving her backbone downward, amber eyes pupil-dilated with a primal, wild look, and his mind took a turn. Maybe she would tell him what she really saw when she looked at that ungrown nigger. He imagined Elizabeth and Hotshot sitting side by side on the floor of a boxcar. They were watching a coupling of cats, to a quickening rattle of the rails and blows of a train whistle. Swallowed up by the motion and the rhythm, they were fascinated by the orgasmic tenor of it all, maybe even aroused by it. Maybe they had felt it before. Josephine rolled over again on the office floor, pawing her feet at the air, then over again, to raise the vulval offering high as she mewed, deep and long. He stood, leaned over her, reaching with both hands, getting both hands around her neck, squeezing tight and lifting fast. And just as fast, before the animal could get claw the first in him, Royce flip-flopped her body over with a circular swing of his arms, feeling the snap of the spine's crack from the cat's skull, Josephine limp and heavy in his grasp, dead weight hitting the floor. He walked into the bathroom and opened a cabinet beneath the sink. He found a croaker sack there and raked the lifeless feline into it, unapologetic, unsympathetic, and unaware of the lifelessness within himself.

He wasn't sorry for his mama, "Moaning Mona Anne," never for one second bought her story that she had to get money to support him, that there was no other way when times were so bad for everybody. He wasn't sorry for Hotshot. Lost from his daddy? It was probably more like his daddy lost him on purpose, saw through that retard act and knew he was a lunatic likely to do somebody in one day. And Josephine? He wasn't one bit sorry that goddamn cat was dead. Elizabeth would sure as hell never have to know and if the sheriff ever figured out what he did, well, Old Man Lacey would probably thank him for solving the population problem. Royce smiled and reached down to grasp the rough weave of the fabric into a tight bunch, bringing it up off the deep brown hardwood floor, straightening his body and his sense of purpose. He slung the sack over his shoulder and headed for the bridge over Cane Creek.

Looking for John David Vines

Christy Logan looked across and around the dim interior of the Palomino Lounge outside Columbus, Mississippi, as she and her best friend Malia took up residence at a round table off to the side. The crowd was sparse, as it was not yet mid-afternoon. The pool balls clicked against each other, cue heels thudded against the concrete floor and punctuated muted country classics. She inventoried the scattered knots of faces. No JD. But she had sensed he would not be here. Still, she searched through the scattered wisps of smoke and hazy light from Christmas strings stapled to the ceiling, trying not to let her disappointment show. She waved at Miller Sams, the bartender. "Send us two Bud Lights," she half-hollered. She had dated Miller five years earlier and liked to believe he was still not over her, liked to believe that none of them ever really got over her, intoxicating as her effect upon men was known to be.

Malia fidgeted and squirmed her broadening ass into a chair with a curved back. She had crossed into the territory of her thirties with a surrendering nod to her thunderous thighs and fat-dimpled behind that Christy could not fathom. Malia was married, though, and happily, or so it seemed. Sometimes her husband, Dewey, joined them at the clubs, but mostly he stayed in front of the TV rigging his rods and reels when he wasn't working at the car lot. And he never seemed to mind that his wife went out with Christy to the bars. Most married men would raise a fuss about that. Maybe he figured no one would find his wife attractive enough to hit on, especially with Christy around; or maybe he really did trust her to keep her vows. Christy herself was twenty-nine, just beginning to steel her ego against the foray into the next decade of her life, suddenly a-panic that she was singular as opposed to plural, an "I" rather than an "us." In that regard, she secretly envied her friend.

Malia lit a cigarette, a Capri menthol 120, and held it between her nails, sculpted and red, like patent leather under the pointed bits of light. She exhaled a rushing cloud of smoke. "Well," she said, smirking, "I had to shave Dewey's butt last night."

"Did not!" Christy drew her nose into a deep crinkle of disgust.

"Oh, honey, yeah," Malia said. "And I'm here to tell you that is one hairy man."

"God!"

"Took a pile of hair off that man's ass this high." She held her palm four inches above the table top. "I'm 'on start calling him Sasquatch."

"Gag me one time, why don't you," Christy said, maintaining the nose crinkle.

"Well, shit, it was the only way I could get at those carbuncles. He's got three of the damn things scattered all over his butt. Has to sit on a ring of foam rubber like he's got hemorrhoids or something."

"That's what you get for marrying a man ten years older than you."

"It ain't no big deal."

"God, I couldn't be married—all the time having to do gross shit like that," Christy said, reappraising her rush at the altar. But JD wouldn't have carbuncles. JD was too handsome and polished to need his butt shaved, ever.

"Aaah." Malia flipped the back of her hand and shrugged as Vicky the waitress set two beers down on the table.

"How y'all doing?" Vicky said.

"Just barely," Malia said.

Christy leaned forward, waiting to seize an opportunity to ask about JD.

"Where's that crazy husband of yours?"

"Hell," Malia said and drew on her skinny little cigarette. "He's laid up at the house, legs all swole up with the gout."

"I thought it was the carbuncles had him down."

"Honey, no. On top of the carbuncles, he's flat laid out on the bed with his shit swole up."

"Gross."

"Hell, that man is a train wreck. Just a pile of writhing misery."

"And I see you ain't at home a-holding his hand," Vicky said.

"Are you serious? Cause you know I don't give up my

nights out. But I told him he could just as easy set his ass on that foam rubber ring and prop his legs up in a bar as he could at home. Sometimes he just likes to be miserable. But, hey, that don't mean I got to be."

"Ain't you even going to cook him no dinner?" Vicky asked.

Christy peeled at the Bud Light label, growing antsy and impatient with the conversation.

"Shit, I asked him what did he want and I'd go to the store and get it. I would've cooked him a pile of chicken or a steak, anything. But he was being all pitiful and puny, trying to get me to feel sorry for him, said he didn't want nothing but some Popsicles. Ain't that fucked up? So I went to the Food Tiger, got four goddamn boxes of fucking Popsicles, shoved them in the freezer, and went on my merry little way. Ain't that just some flat-out fucked up shit?"

"But if he's got the gout, how—"

"Hey Vicky," Christy interjected. "You seen JD this afternoon?"

Vicky's left eyebrow twitched upward. "Careful, honey."

"Come on. Has he been by here?"

"No, he ain't. Sorry. Or, hell, maybe I ain't sorry. You ought to give that man a wide way to go."

"Did I ask your opinion?"

"Okay, okay. Just remember who said it." She carried the round wooden tray back over to the bar.

"See? Somebody else agrees with me. John David Vines is a womanizing son of a bitch and ain't even about to leave his wife."

"Shut up! Don't nobody know what's between us. Nobody. We got a deep history together." Christy let her green eyes toss out the quintessential bitch gaze that had been one of her staples throughout the last half of her twenties. It was a look that had sent more than one man into a blundering marathon of ass-kissing apologies and more that one woman into a fetal, tear-infested restroom retreat. And it had its desired effect upon Malia Dobbins.

"So are we going to stay here?" Malia asked.

"Long enough for this beer. Then we'll try some other bars."

"And he said for sure he'd meet you?"

"I told you already what he said. He said he'd do his best to get out this afternoon, that he'd borrow a car so his wife couldn't find him, that he'd run by the usual places. He said we'd talk about things."

"Things?"

"Yeah, things. Important things." Christy took a long swallow of beer. Her first romance with John David Vines was when she was nineteen, working as a teller at the First National Bank during the day, spending weekends at the bars, dancing to honky-tonk rock bands, learning how to use the power she was discovering she had over men. She had always been noticed for her looks, the black-haired, green-eyed, bold-breasted looks of a bar-girl queen. She was drafted to hand out the trophy every Sunday at the Dirt Track Races, and at the Flat Track Race every Thursday night. She ran for Watermelon Queen and won in a landslide. When she walked into a bar, men hollered her name, bought her drinks, and talked louder than usual; women either maneuvered into her small circle of girlfriends or watched her from across the bar, downing drinks and jealousy, but hoping to capture some of the magic.

John David Vines was one of the first to get deep into her panties. He had magic of his own. He was four years older, a boy she had watched on the football field when she was a freshman in high school, not yet pushed out at the breasts and hips. JD was golden and blonde with an edgy attitude that drew the attention of the kind of females who liked to taste danger. He never noticed Christy in high school, but when he came back to town after a stint in the Army he could not overlook the hottest girl in any club, and he courted her, ran his tongue along her neck and pulled her red underwear aside to touch her with the kind of knowledge the other boys did not begin to have.

She was not a slut, though, did not honor just anyone with that regal warmth between her bronzed thighs. She had lost her virginity to a blundering, pencil-dicked baseball player back in the eleventh grade and decided not to hand it out to anyone who did not show a plethora of potential. Which made her all the more desirable, since those few males who had that honor bestowed upon them could pass in the knowledge that she had knighted them in recognition of their sexual prowess. And everybody else knew it, too. Other women were intrigued when they heard who was Christy Logan's latest all the way man; consequently, for that chosen man even more pussy became available, increasing exponentially with each score thereafter. It was the strongest reference one could hope for.

She managed to keep herself from giving in to JD for a long time, though, in spite of his practiced fingers. She only let him put it in part way, at first, keeping him fevered and amped up on hormones. She had him where she loved to get men, on the teetering edge of potential ecstasy, where they filled her head with lush words, Mississippi sonnets of desire, and odes to her heart-pumping presence. She feasted on the rush of it all until it played out, most times growing tired of it after a while, moving on to the next man without ever letting the current one put it all the way in. But JD had a way with his touch and it was only a matter of time before her long, tanned legs were slung around his back, thighs sliding in a slick rhythm that snatched all sense of control away from her, leaving her the one wanting more, her sexual compass in pieces on the floor. It was too, too, frightening, and she quickly broke it off, breaking his heart, scoffing at his pleas to get married and have his babies, moving on to the next rush of power.

Christy rode the wild-child, hot-chick reputation for several years without slipping into slut-dom, but the latter part of her twenties found her reflection in the fluorescent-lit bathroom mirrors more hardened and drawn with precursor wrinkles. She married briefly, at twenty-seven, to an older man who had a little money and premature ejaculations that left her irritated by his ineptitude, left her spitting disgusted words at him until she realized he wasn't worth what little wealth he had. But she was married long enough to have a baby, a little boy who reminded her too much of his wimp of a daddy, a little boy who was now being raised by her mother. The thing that had grown in her left scarred stretch marks on her stomach and thighs, gave her breasts too much of a sag to tolerate. She got herself some implants, "store bought titties," Malia called them, and stepped inch by inch toward a metamorphosis into that which she had resisted up until now, up until she took up with a married man and ex-love named John David Vines. She knew, deep in the back of her head, that she was just before turning into a bar skank.

✳

The crowd at the 45 Club was ushering in the after five spirit, thick with conversation and laughter. Christy and Malia had executed passes through the Three Pigs, Peggy's, and The S Curve, feeling the growing swell of happy hour with each stop, giggling more easily with the friends and acquaintances they encountered.

"Y'all know Godzilla Dobbins, don't you?" Malia asked a group clustered by the bar at the S Curve. "She's my monster-in-law, Dewey's mama. She hates my guts but she's the one got us together in the first place."

Oakley Starnes, Tim Hilyer and Tedder Bumpus, all friends of Dewey's, chuckled at the reference.

"That old woman is mean enough to scare the buggers out of a bugger-bear," Tim said.

"No shit," Malia said. "Still and all, she brung us together. It was back when Dewey was dating this Pentecostal churchwoman, you know, Babs Elmore. She was one of them Walking Elmores that used to walk up and down the highway of a day, walk to town, walk to the next county. Anyway, she took up with a Pentecostal Church, then she took up with Dewey, then she broke his heart. And you know what Dewey's mama said?"

"Naw."

"Tell it, then."

"Godzilla said, 'Boy you need to quit mopin' and moanin' around the house, laying all over the sofa eating up the cushions with your butt crack.' She said, 'Son, forget about that church woman and go on out to a bar somewhere and find you a nice woman that'll make you happy.' Ain't that some shit?"

Christy let laughter and smoke billow up around her thoughts about JD.

"Old Dewey's stove up, huh?" Tedder asked.

"God, yes. Got the gout and the butt carbuncles, and—I forgot to tell you this, Christy—he's got some seed ticks in his head that's been living there since he went hunting in the woods last Tuesday evening and won't let me pull them out."

"How do you keep from puking at all the shit you have to do for that man?" Christy said.

"It ain't nothing, really. But I admit I like to fell out and fainted when he showed me them seed ticks and said we was going to have to let them suck on his scalp a while till they get big enough to grab a-holt of."

"I pulled one the size of a big raisin off my wife's head not long ago," Tim said.

"Gag a maggot," Christy said. "Look here."

"No, you look here," Tedder said. "Come on and dance with me, Christy."

"I ain't in a dancing mood." Tedder was also a high school friend who had always harbored a crush on her, as did many of the other boys she grew up with.

He leaned close to her ear. "One day," he said. "One day you going to let me touch it, ain't you?"

She punched him hard in the arm. "Have any of y'all seen JD?" she asked.

Oakley cleared his throat. Tim looked down at the floor. "I know y'all have."

"Naw, we ain't. Really," Tim said. "Go on and dance

with Tedder. Give him a thrill."

"I said I ain't in a dancing mood."

"Remember the time old Dewey put that bull catfish in the wading pool?" Oakley said.

"Oh, hell, now that was some fuuucked uuuup shit," Malia drew the words out long. "He was so fucking proud of that big-ass fish that he blew up this blue plastic wading pool we keep in the shed for our little nephew. Then he called up Bobby Pollins because Bobby had told him he wasn't no kind of fisherman. He just had to show the damn thing to Bobby, you know, so he could make like he had a dick after all."

Christy pushed her thumbnail against the label on the beer bottle, under the gummy-wet side of it, against the cold moisture.

"But Bobby didn't come over till the next morning and that fish stayed in that little blowed up pool all night, and it was February, you know, and the temperature dropped."

The men laughed, threw their heads back, then bent forward in a rhythm of humor.

"So Dewey got all puffed up, so proud of this big fat dick hanging between his legs, and walked Bobby round back to look at the fish. But the water had done froze and that fish was laid over on its side, just wall-eyed dead. And I guess poor old Dewey's pecker shriveled up like a old pea hull or something, but all he said was, 'I reckon I need to go on and skin that one, don't I?' Poor thing."

The laughter wrapped them all, until Christy punched through it, tearing at the label on her beer bottle. "Where the hell did y'all see JD? Huh?"

"To hell with JD," Tim said, grabbing Christy's forearm

and pulling her over to the small dance floor near a jukebox that fuzzed out a Randy Travis song.

"Why you want to be grabbing me like that?"

"Cause you make me lose control, baby," he said, laughing.

"Why do y'all change the subject whenever I mention JD?"

He pulled her in to his body and they moved to the slow country rhythm. He leaned his lips close to her ear, sending tickles of air down the flesh of her neck. "I get jealous when I'm trying to impress a woman and all she does is go on about some other man."

"You are full of shit."

He straightened up to look her hard and steady in the eyes, a look ripe with interest, coaxing her intrigue. "Am I?" And he pulled her in again, arms encircling her, tightening, every subtle ripple of muscle against muscle telling her the tide was turning, honky-tonk currents were swirling past, threatening to carry her down under.

She wanted to throw a smart remark in his face, toss her hair back, do her bitch walk away from him, but she just as much wanted to finish the dance, nice as it felt to forget about JD, if only for a few minutes. So she let him push his knee between her thighs, breathe into her neck, stroke his palm down her back until it glanced the upper regions of her ass. But when the music ended, the panic set in as never before, so she lifted her eyes to meet his, squinted hard and mean. "You," she said again, this time with an index finger pressed to his chest, "are full of shit." She strode over to the table, gathered up her purse and Malia, and they headed out for the next bar.

※

The ladies' room at Martin's River House Club had four stalls and a bank of sinks backed by a big mirror. Flushing rushes of water, the clunk-clunk of the paper towel dispenser and gossip-toned conversation echoed against tiled walls.

"This is the nicest john of all the bars," Malia observed as she touched up her makeup. "Too bad the damn club sucks." She had been acting a shade different since they left the 45 Club, close-mouthed, but now she engaged in restroom girl talk.

"You told that right," came from Jennifer Gainus, who was bent over, head down, brushing her thick-curled hair. She straightened up fast, throwing her hair out in a puffy fluff of spiraling waves. "Only reason I come here is to see is anything going on, just in case there is, just to check it off the list and move on, you know?"

Christy contorted her lips into a tight 'o' and re-coated them with frosty bronze lipstick before blotting them with a square of toilet paper. "So have you seen JD?"

Malia rolled her eyes.

"Not lately. I seen him last night at the Playmore." Jennifer crimped and pulled at her hair, bringing it farther out from her head.

"Damn, girl, if you hair gets any bigger you're going to have to steal the Sasquatch title off of Dewey."

Jennifer laughed, then let her voice get fierce and low with the promise of a newsy tidbit. "I have to tell y'all, though, what I heard about Tim Hilyer."

Christy's level of interest doubled. "Yeah? We was just with him."

"Well, he's on the make, wife or no wife, so be careful. My sister-in-law seen him out back of the Playmore last night, back behind the dumpster, getting himself a blow job from damn Screwsie Dawson."

"Goddamn," Christy breathed. "He ain't just on the make. He's sunk way the hell down."

"No shit," Malia said. "What I hear is guys go back for more of them Dawson blow jobs cause if she really likes you she takes out her upper plate."

The three of them let squealing laughter echo up the tiled walls. Then Jennifer dug through her purse for a compact. "You better watch JD's wife don't get wind of the two of you, though, Christy."

"Shit. She'll know before long, and she ought to know by now. I been leaving clues behind lately."

"You are crazy, girl."

"Seriously," Christy said.

"What in the holy hell you been leaving?" Malia asked.

"Oh, just little things. A earring here, a Kleenex with my lip color on it there, but she's so dumb she ain't figured it out yet."

"Hell, if you want her to know, just call the bitch up," Jennifer said.

"That'd just make JD mad. No, the clues I'm leaving could be, like, accidental, you know? He couldn't get mad about that."

"So she ain't picked up on any of them clues, huh?"

"Hell no. That must be one dumb as dirt woman. Shit, I'd leave one of my thongs in the car but she'd probably just pick it up, take it for a Scrunchy, and put her damn hair up with it."

A fresh wave of giggles bounced from the lavatory walls, as the three women shared more bits of gossip. Malia did an impersonation of Dewey trying to see his butt in the mirror and the giggles were magnified in volume. The three of them chatted, primped, and preened, making ready to move on to the next club, hoping for another drama or two, perhaps even their own.

✳

The parking lot at the Playmore Lounge was almost full when they turned in around seven-thirty. A Dangerous Thing, one of the local dance bands, would be playing tonight, but not until nine, and would go until one or two. JD always showed up at the Playmore at some point of an evening, just like everybody who frequented bars on the back side of town. At once it occurred to Christy that JD had never offered to meet her at the Ramada Lounge or the Montclair, or any of the bars where a more upscale, professional crowd gathered. She had frequented those bars fairly regularly before JD, but they only met at the rough-around-the-edges places where he would not be seen by his wife's friends.

Christy glanced over at Malia, who had gone quiet once again—for her, an aberration. A few clusters of folks were scattered about the parking lot. A young couple made out against the passenger's side of a Toyota. Jukeboxed music rode the neon glow lighting their car's interior in a haze of red. "I don't want to get out here yet. Let's just drive around some."

"Alright," Malia sighed. "But I'm a couple of beers into my buzz. Don't let me fuck up in front of a goddamn squad car."

"You're doing fine."

"For now, I guess. Where you want to go? To the bar at Sipsey?"

"Hell, no. You saw the Simms boys' pulpwood truck there and you know JD ain't going nowhere them Simmses are hanging out. Every time he runs into them he breaks a pool cue over somebody's head."

"No shit. Them Simmses ain't good for nothin' but the four F's: fuckin', fightin', and fixin' flats." She gave Christy a suspicious sideways glance. "So where you want to go?"

"Drive down the strip, okay?"

Malia looked at her then with a sudden expression that Christy had never experienced, so buffeted as she had always been by beauty and desirability. It was an expression of concern, even pity, and it took her breath with its quick intensity. "You don't want to do this, hon."

"Goddamn, don't look at me like that. I just want to see is his car at any of the restaurants on the strip."

"We ain't never gone chasing him down when he was with his family. That's over the line. That ain't right."

Christy slapped the dashboard with her right palm, hard. "I ain't chasing him down. Just go the hell to the strip and drive through the Wendy's and the McDonald's and whatever the hell other burger joints and restaurants you see."

"Okay, okay. But I ain't getting out and neither are you. If you want to make a scene, save it for the Playmore. Not in front of no damn young-uns."

"I ain't stupid."

Malia said nothing. She put the car in drive and turned out of the parking lot, onto the highway back to Columbus.

When Christy had first confronted her reflection in the mirror after the birth of the baby, she had collapsed in a sobbing heap on the hospital floor. It was too much. The dimpled flesh of her stomach was supposed to be flat and firm, a backdrop for the sexy emerald navel ring she wore. And her hipbones! They had fanned out, widening her lower body. Her whole skeletal and muscular ecology, it seemed, had been upset. Her breasts were swollen huge and hard with milk that seeped from her nipples, leaving round wet spots on her nightgown. Once emptied, those breasts spilled lower against her chest. It had taken almost a year and a good chunk of money to coax her body back into the kind of shape she could bear to show a man, and just in time for JD. JD told her she was beautiful, that his wife had let herself go after having their two children. JD kissed her stomach, told her stretch marks were a badge of honor, like the scar on his chest from being cut in a bar fight when he was stationed at Ft. Benning. He called her store-bought titties magnificent, reassured her that she was the most lovely, most luscious woman he had ever known or could ever hope to know. Where he had known just the right touches to her flesh in their early romance, he now knew just the right words to say to her flagging, aging ego.

✳

His car was parked at the Mexican Kitchen, his favorite restaurant. Malia had ridden her around the vinyl-lined, playgrounded drive-thrus of every ticky-tacky fast food joint on the strip before it occurred to Christy that he might have picked a place he liked better. Malia pulled into the parking lot across the street from the restaurant that was roof-topped with a life-sized team of heavy plastic horses pulling a wagon.

One of the horses had fallen over, its white plastic legs stuck sideward, like a carcass ripe with rigor mortis. The stucco building spilled light through two glass doors and a bank of windows on the upper level. Christy and Malia sat smoking Capri cigarettes, like partner cops on a stakeout.

After the second cigarette, Malia sighed. "This is boring. Let's go back to the bar and dance."

The bitch look came across Christy's face with authority.

"Well the plan was to have a good time. Dewey's probably having a better time than we are, him all laid up, even."

"That's his car. It can't be much longer."

"Only a lifetime."

"What kind of a friend says that? How come you want to say things like that to me?" Christy threw her cigarette through the open window, something in her emotional gut telling her she should not have asked.

Malia put both hands on the steering wheel, looked thoughtful for a moment, then turned her face to her friend. "Tedder told me, when you was off dancing with Hilyer, that JD's been avoiding you like crazy."

"You're lying." Christy felt cornered, hemmed in, desperate. "You don't know what's between us."

"Honey, JD ain't worth all this. Tedder said—"

"Tedder said shit. Tedder Bumpus is a dumb-ass redneck from Gordo who—"

She stopped, the parking lot's light hitting her arms as she leaned forward, palms on the dashboard.

JD strolled through the glass door of the Mexican Kitchen and out into the open night air. He was followed by two small boys, dark-haired little boys maybe six and seven years of age; running, rambunctious little boys who wrestled and horse-played their way across the pavement and into their daddy's car. JD leaned against the hood and lit a cigarette, his muscular frame bathed in fluorescence.

Christy reached for the door handle, but Malia leaned all the way across her taking her wrist. "I ain't letting you do that, honey," she said in a soft voice.

Christy was crying, had not realized it, but now she knew she was crying, watching JD lean against the hood of his car, smoking like a cocky, never-caught thief.

"Let's go." Malia reached for the keys.

"No," Christy said, still watching as a woman approached JD, a plump woman with dark hair, who Christy knew was his wife. And the plump woman took the cigarette from his lips and thumped it out onto the highway. JD laughed and grabbed the woman, twisting her arm playfully behind her back and the woman was laughing, too. Then one of the little boys stuck his head out the back seat window and JD let go of the plump woman and pretended a punch toward the boy, who ducked back inside the car. And before the woman walked around the car she looked up at JD and said something that made him throw his head back and laugh like Christy had never, ever seen him laugh. He was still laughing and shaking his head when the passenger's side door closed.

Malia had her arm around Christy through the whole of the scene in the parking lot, Christy's eyeliner and mascara smudged and smearing as she rubbed at hot tears. Then she stopped, abruptly, bitch-look overtaking vulnerability, overriding it as unacceptable, an effigy giving in to the first real gulp of a bitterness she had barely tasted up until now. "Get me the hell away from here," Christy said, "before I kill his ass."

*

The Playmore was rocking. A Dangerous Thing covered songs like "Strokin'" and "Knock on Wood," classic songs that pulled folks onto the dance floor, but the band was taking a break by the time make-up was refreshed and emotions packed away. Christy and Malia found themselves reunited with Tedder, Oakley, and Tim, who had made their way there via Burt's Game Room, where they had seen Joey Taggart and Sonny Sams get into a vicious fist fight in the parking lot, a fight during which Sonny kicked Joey's butt for telling lies on Sonny's girlfriend.

"Good," Malia said. "I never did like Joey Taggart. He ain't nothing but one of them long, tall, raw-boned fellers with a headache for a face."

"Well, it's one messed up face right about now," Tim said. He turned to Christy. "You're mighty quiet, girl."

She gave him here practiced glare. "I was just thinking."

"About what?"

"About how stupid men are to fight over women, for women, about women."

"Shit. We'll do just about anything for pussy. And y'all know it."

"Ain't that the truth," Tedder said. "Hell, Lisa said that old man Christy was married to would get so beside hisself he'd water the furrow before he could even go to plowing."

Christy rolled her eyes. "Don't remind me."

"Hey, Malia, what about you? Will old Dewey jump through hoops for that good stuff?"

"He's a man, ain't he?"

Christy was glad to let her carry the conversation now,

now that she had gotten her answer to the question of the evening. Malia went on, holding forth. "Dewey's so horny all I got to do is aim it in his direction and he's all over it. Or he'll say, 'Baby, why don't you put on them "fuck-me" pumps and crawl up in the covers with a tired old man.' Ain't that some shit?"

"He ain't real romantic, huh," Tedder said.

"Dewey Dixon? I'll tell you Dewey's idea of romance. He called me from work one afternoon a couple of weeks ago and said, 'Dust off that ol' puss, Baby, cause I'm coming home for a sardine sammich and then I'm fixing to lay some pipe up in there.' And that man didn't understand why I just went on to the Food Tiger, went on about my business, carried my mama her hormone prescription, didn't give him another thought. Had his bottom lip all run out by the time I got home."

Malia's audience laughed, swapped Stupid Romance Trick stories while Christy let it all become nothing more that air rushing at her ears, air becoming the angry sound of the ocean, as if she were ear-muffed by two big conch shells. She wished the band would start up again. She wanted to dance, to move, to feel as wild and beautiful as she had as a teenager. She wanted to lean her body into Tim Hilyer's and make him want her more than any wife could ever be wanted, and she let her eyes go to his. The group was still talking, laughing, mouths moving soundlessly in the smoky dimness, but Tim's eyes cut to hers more and more frequently, sending her a look she knew. She smiled him an answer, then slid her glance away.

At the bar, Wendel Mitchell was serving up beer after beer, filling trays for Gail, Jo-Jo, and Katrina, the three

Saturday night waitresses. Colored lights danced around the Playmore's huge party room, and the clusters of faces were like photo images of the faces Christy had seen here last week. It never changed much. Most of the men at the bar had occupied the same barstools for years, and the predictability of their attitudes, of the music and fights and soap operas playing out from night to night kept fear at bay, for a little while. At the far end of the bar Susie Dawson stood between the legs of Karl Thornton, her palms rubbing his outer thighs. Karl's divorce was final and he was looking to get laid, Christy figured. And it wouldn't be difficult with Screwsie Dawson staking a claim there in the shadow of his crotch.

Somewhere through the padded silence Christy finally heard the electric buzz of a bass guitar, the rattle of drumsticks against a snare and a cymbal as the musicians took their places. There was a picking and tuning of strings, a random strike or two at the drums. Then, finally, a blending of rhythms into a tune and the gentle rock of singing guitars. A slow song, another old dance standard, "My Girl." She had danced with JD so many times to that very song and he could go to hell as far as she was concerned. A sting of tears tried to rise up to her closed eyes now, as she pressed against Tim's chest, her cheek against his shoulder, moving with him on the dance floor. She slid her arms up and around his neck, fingertips brushing the flesh of the back of his neck, and when he pushed his lips against her own neck the warmth of his kisses took her. She would be alright if only she could have another shot, another chance, and she would go on peeling the labels off beer bottles for however long it took. She squeezed the back of Tim's neck, pushed her hips forward, let her crotch rub a tempo against his thigh. She would try for as long as she had to, beginning with Tim Hillyer. And she didn't care if her fingernails went to nubs from peeling back labels as long as she could have another shot at that which she kept cloaked in fragile power and musky promises, the kind of love she craved and hoarded and inevitably hurled away.

The Fall of the Nixon Administration

In light of my current situation with the law, I suppose it's a good thing I did not shoot Will Luckie in the back of the head when I had the chance. After all, if folks are going to get all tore up over the demise of a few pullets, then there surely would have been a mighty hew and cry over Will's demise—even though he is no better than any of the yard fowl I exploded with my dead daddy's—"D.D." for short in our family—Remington Model 1100 12 gauge automatic. And I refuse to say otherwise, even if they put hot lights in my face, withhold food and water, interrogate me for days on end, or attempt to beat any endearing words out of me. Will Luckie has single-handedly brought down the Calhouns and I will never forgive him.

You need to know that Will Luckie is a descendant of the mouth breathers who live out the Pipeline Road, where they pass their beer-ridden days hauling pulpwood, screwing one another's wives, and having an occasional trailer burning to collect enough insurance money to buy more beer and pulpwood trucks. He is through and through Florida Panhandle white trash—pure carrion—and ever since he entered our once picture-perfect lives, I have been subjected to his low-class ways.

First off, he keeps a pouch of Beechnut in the front pocket of his double knit shorts, which makes for a rather unnerving bulge that is, at best, in bad taste, and, at worst, just plain lewd. And he knows it. To be thoroughly honest, he rarely, if ever, wears underwear. I can safely say this because of the revealing nature of sand-colored double knit; it just does not afford the barrier as does, say, denim, or heavy cotton. And when the heightened level of sexual arousal that has settled upon my mother's abode is thrown into the mix—well, let me just say that I am quite certain—and I apologize for being so graphic—but it is more than obvious that the smarmy little gigolo is not even circumcised.

Plus, he spits. He spits that stinking concoction between his index and third finger, pulling his lips taut and skeeting that mess out in high, arching streaks of amber. His presence, ergo his spittle, here at Mimi's house, which has always been the showplace home in Pollard, has cheapened the entire property right along with the Calhoun name. At present there are tobacco juice stains dotted across Mother's patios, in puddles next to the ornamental urns, down the stone walkway that once wound so pleasantly among the pines, and all around the swimming pool where he passes the days sunning and sipping fruity drinks of gin bearing paper umbrellas. Lord knows, at this precise second three of mother's Waterford Crystal tumblers hold a few ounces of that nauseating looking, tobacco-infused saliva. I have even regularly found one of Grandma Lucie's sterling silver goblets perched on the toilet tank, floating those little black flecks across a phlegm-glazed surface of bubbly brown spit. I have told Will Luckie repeatedly how repugnant it looks. He laughs every time. "Tell it to Bob Haldeman," he says, laughing.

My God, how he laughs! He laughed when I told him to wear a shirt to Mother's surprise birthday luncheon last month. Knowing that the leading citizens of Pollard would be there, taking mental notes on the progress of Mother's debauched incapacitation. He laughed and said that if he was going to stand around the pool nibbling cocktail weenies with a bunch of tight-assed holy rollers, he had to be prepared to bail at any second. Thus, the aforementioned double knit shorts. And the chest hair with those hideous gold chains garlanded into it like some kind of pornographic Christmas tree. And yes, he did at one point do a cannonball into the water, which soaked the fondue table and Mayor Burgess's wife Kathryn's silk skirt. And when Will Luckie emerged from the water it was painfully obvious that the famous nude shorts he wore were also soaked, displaying yet another level of phallic information we did not require; the energy that went into avoiding eye contact with his vile, blue-veined interloper would be enough to fuel all the paper mills in this county. I have never been more mortified. That is how much he cares about making the right impression with influential people. Plus, he even threatened to invite John and Martha Mitchell to the party to strew feathers hither and yon. Instead, he rounded up Charles Colson, a Buff Orpington and his favorite, and, as an encore, proceeded to introduce him to the guests, all the while stroking him and making absurd little kissy noises at him.

The thing that absolutely stuns me is that people—even well-bred ones—seem to like him, up to a point, contrary to all personal moral codes, as they surely must object to his gene pool and his flimflamming of my mother. Maybe it is because he drags out that cheap guitar and sings country songs with a disturbingly rich voice or tells those "humorous anecdotes" that always eventually descend into the blue depths of hardcore porn. Maybe it is that subtle layer of pansexuality that seems to intrigue both genders in spite of themselves. Maybe it is the Newman-blue eyes, the dimply Kirk Douglas smile, or the George Hamilton tan-lacquered physique, enhanced by his two decades in the Marine Corps. No matter. I consider him the idiot savant of a Svengali, who tapped into Mother's sense of herself as a poet. Mother should have lived the life of an artistic expatriate rather than "atrophying" here in Pollard. She never did appreciate her status.

Status. The state of us. There is the crux of it, as far as I am concerned. Mother has called me shallow, but civic responsibility should never, in my opinion, be taken for granted. You cannot fully appreciate this whole fiasco unless you understand that the Calhouns are the single most prominent of the three most prominent families in Pollard, which is prominent in itself as the county seat. "We occupy the penultimate position of prominence," Mother used to like to say, given her penchant for alliteration. Because of this, and out of a sheer sense of civic duty, I am President of the Ladies' Club, parliamentarian of the DAR, Brownie scout troop leader at the Methodist Church, Sunday School class coordinator at the Baptist Church, and I would have beat out Bitsy Burgess Swafford, the mayor's evil daughter, as president of the Daughters of the Confederacy, if not for the shame of Will Luckie. As it is, I feel that my genetic destiny as a community leader has slipped. If I had chosen to do nothing, it could have taken years to rebuild the family name; so I did something about it, albeit apparently too much to ever hope to repair the Calhoun name now. And Mother? Mother simply fails to care one whit about the shambled legacy she has foisted upon me.

You see, my DD's DD was a circuit judge who survived The Crash and three bouts of cancer before he died of age; naturally, he knew everybody and all their legal business. My DD was a banker with the foresight to buy all the timber land and mineral rights he could get his hands on so naturally he knew everybody's financial business. He was a philanderer and died of gallstones. My husband, Winston Dozier (though try as I might, I can only contextualize myself as a Calhoun) is a physician—the only one in town besides Dr. Dave, who is ancient—and Winston knows everybody's personal business so it does not matter that he is a tad prissy for a man. And my mother is from an extremely well regarded political family in Birmingham, Alabama. Did you know that right this second her brother is some Big Ike in the Nixon administration? Hell, she and Daddy went to the first inauguration—and the main ball, not any of the little rinky-dink ones. And she acts like it is no big deal that the Nixon administration is falling into a mangled heap, running around like a bunch of decapitated biddies. So you see, she could know everybody's political business if she had the inclination. On top of that, it is said that she is the wealthiest woman in three counties, thanks to her DD and my DD. And after just shy of a year of mourning my daddy, what does she do? She takes herself a boyfriend twenty-two years and seven months her junior—making him four full months younger than me—and sets all the town's tongues to wagging about my own family's familial business.

Are you beginning to fathom why Will Luckie might be so intrigued with my withering up old mama? And why I have so much to lose?

Of course, I have attempted to be fair where Will Luckie is concerned. It simply would not be Christ-like to do otherwise. I am the first to concede that Mother is not, well, "ordinary" is the adjective that comes to mind. She is a bit of an eccentric, as so many of the wealthy are, and she has always been fond of drama. She is not above pressing a palm to her chest or the back of a hand to her forehead and uttering plaintive little bleats of suffering peppered with curses. Mother can swear with the fluency of a wounded sailor. Naturally, her dramas and her imminent death are all in her head; Dr. Dave has been giving her sugar pills for years. And me? Well, I am the devoted daughter, childless, without siblings, with only a limp-wristed Baptist husband to help with my mother and her shiftless little slut of a boyfriend. Now don't get me wrong, I heartily embrace my daughterly duties. Heaven knows, I have never failed to be at her side when she was mid-crisis, even throughout the hypochondriacal frenzy of her golden years, living with my husband in the shadow of Mother's big white-columned three-story. Many are the times I have delivered satin bed jackets and Merle Norman cosmetics to her hospital rooms, spoon fed her while that popping jaw of hers nearly sent me over the precipice and into a ranting, maniacal conniption fit, and taken all the verbal abuse I should have to stomach in five lifetimes.

"CeCe, I cannot bear the thought of dying without seeing you living your life," she says. "Run off to Nepal, for God's sake! Go to a goddamn nude beach in Europe. Have an affair in Lisbon and breakfast in Madrid. Do not fester and stagnate as I once did." Or: "Cecelia LaRue, you have no hunger for life. Where is the passion you should have inherited from me? Jumping Jesus, if you would just come alive you would begin to claw at this provincial little coffin of a town." Which is just a pure and solid lie. She was perfectly content with her life BWL (Before Will Luckie).

"She overshadows you," my DD used to say. "You've got to learn to talk louder, act meaner, and cuss dirtier than she does." Easy for him to say, with his bourbons and baseball. With his hunting camp whores and wooded weekends. But it simply is not in my nature to be overbearing like Mother. On the contrary, I feel that I should project an image of calm competence and ladylike strength, what with my position and all. Heaven knows, I have even been called a saint by some who have observed my devotion to Mother.

Our maid Lindia only calls me a fool. She has even gone so far as to tell me she thinks I should get a new husband. "One that don't swish," she says. "Leave Pollard, and let the chips fall." Lindia even thinks Mother should be allowed to have her way with this—"character" of hers. "She deserves him," Lindia says. "She went long years not getting none from your running around daddy. Well, she's damn sure getting plenty now."

But I cannot let it go. Not when the whole town is

watching and talking and looking at me with the false pity of peons who just eat up a good, high-society scandal with the same sticky spoon. Not when Mother and Will Luckie go on trips to India and Morocco, come back loaded down with expensive trinkets, ivory, rich fur pillows, hand-woven rugs—my God, her home decor has become a bohemian ode to the Kama Sutra. And of course you know who is paying for these trips and trinkets: yours truly. I am not only paying with my birthright, I am paying with my once impeccable reputation. Just listen at a few of the other things that piece of filth has done to cause an avalanche of shame to come cascading down on the Calhoun family:

First of all, he moved in with her after just two movie dates and one dinner date to Rosie O'Grady's in Pensacola. Swept her right off her chubby little size five feet (mine are size nine; she refers to them as "Jesus-Christ-walk-on-water skis"). I believe the off-color line he wooed her with was, "Baby, you sure do make my rat crawl," or something equally disturbing. At least, that's how she tells it, delighting at the gag reflex-inducing reaction she gets from me and anyone else with common decency. No marriage has ever been discussed (as if I could allow that!)—just a craven union of depraved lust and musked-up sin, which in and of itself is all the town ever needed to justify looking down on me.

Second of all, he buys lubricating jelly and female hygiene spray at Mr. Cleo Williams' pharmacy, and I don't have to tell you the lurid tales that swarm around Billy's Barber Shop and the House of Hair in the wake of that. Don't even ask me about the hand-held muscle massager.

Thirdly, I think I already mentioned he laughs at me and runs me down to my face and behind my back. He calls me a "social-climbing flippy-tailed prissite," as if I have to do any climbing. It is just that I do care what certain people think. It's my nature. Yet he says the crudest things to me, obviously intended to wound and provoke, but I usually mange to hold it in, just as I have always done with Mother. "You need to loosen up, girl," he will say. "You got the biggest bug up your butt I ever seen. Must be one of them dung beetles. You need a dose of Uncle Luckie's Root Treatment." Or he leans in close and whispers, "So who's cutting your stove wood? Cause I know your old man ain't got the ax for it."

Winston has even witnessed him toying with me, insulting me, yet my own husband refuses to take up for me. All he will do is bring me samples of knockout pills to settle my nerves then turn around and give Will Luckie all the free medical attention he needs, and then some. Knowing that "Uncle Luckie" doesn't think Winston has any testosterone, all the time asking why Winston and me don't have any babies after six years of marriage. Then, when I try to tell him something like I guess Jesus isn't ready, he says, right in front of Winston, "More like Winnie ain't ready, and he won't be ready unless you get yourself a dildo. Maybe that would turn him on." Then he laughs while Winston blushes. Of course.

"Bet I could take care of Winnie's retreads if he made a little pit stop on my turn." The gall. My mother's boyfriend flirting with my husband! "Hey, Doc," he says. "My dick stays harder than Chinese arithmetic. I need to come in and get it de-pressurized, alright? Just drain off a little fluid."

I swear I am not exaggerating. He continues his slimy talk and his questioning of Winston's virility just because he knows crude behavior is one of my Achilles' heels and my husband's effete demeanor is the other. I already told you Winston is a touch feminine, but that is just the way of some folks with superior breeding. Plus, I always used to say that there's more to a successful marriage than wallowing around in bed linens. But don't try telling that to Mimi or Will Luckie. Their sordid little soiree goes on in front of all of Pollard. Here's what I mean:

In recent years Mother has taken to routinely calling the police department, fire department, or ambulance company when she needs little errands done. Once, at the conclusion of one of her extended hospitalization-slash-vacations, she even phoned up Cheatham Jackson at the colored funeral parlor to drive her the four blocks home, just because the hospital ambulance was out on a call and she simply *had* to get home right that very minute to set up for *mah jongg*. Yet this town's three bored cops—plus assorted paramedics and firemen—seem to get a kick out of it, driving up to the big house, sirens blaring and lights ablaze, to see what the eccentric socialite wants this time. This behavior never used to bother me too much BWL, as it was quite harmless then. Lord knows, I used to sometimes be there to enjoy the company, when Mother would wave the back of her hand at Grady Fortner, a big fat semi-winded paramedic. "No, darling," she would chirp from her multi-pillowed perch beneath the yellow dotted Swiss canopy. "I'm just fine. Really. All I need you to do is run to the kitchen and pour a little Tab over ice."

And he would.

"Run to the liquor store for me, sweetie pie, and pick me up a fifth of Crown. I'm all out and I'm parched as a goddamn nun's drawers."

After a two a.m. call, the honeyed command might go something like, "Be a sugar-doll, won't you, and run downstairs to the garage. I woke up with this feeling of dread that I forgot to extinguish the lights on my automobile. Oh—and if it's necessary, be my precious and check the battery."

But after the arrival of Will Luckie the visitors became more like salivating voyeurs at a peep show in a Bourbon Street sex salon. Lord, they can't get to Mother's fast enough to gather fodder for the next tale they will share at the barber shop, and she never lets them down. Just a few weeks ago, when Mother's hairdresser accidentally fried the hair he was supposed to be touching up with henna highlights, it turned into yet another show for the P.C.P.D.

When I laid eyes on Mother, all done up to perfection except for the frizzled tufts of hair zigging and zagging from her scalp, I briefly hoped it would be the death knell for Will Luckie, scare him off, maybe. After all, she looked like Bozo the Clown with a singed Afro. And mother's looks, which I did not inherit, by the way (I only inherited my place in the pecking order of Pollard), are known to be strikingly beautiful, even at her age and poundage. She has flawless skin, too smooth for wrinkles to appear harsh, and the greenest eyes this side of Vivien Leigh. I, of course, had acne and kept several Pensacola dermatologists in business throughout high school, and I have these washed-out brown eyes. Where Mother is petite, albeit a hair chubby by now, I am a ski-footed Amazon with a thick waist and saddlebag hips. But I have nice hair, a dazzling smile, and a moral character, which is really all that counts.

Anyway, the evening of Mimi's hair frying incident, I sat in the dark with her in the study, waiting for her Man. A strobing of firelight hit her face, playing upon the burned out barbs of frizzed hair. She held a cigarette in her left hand, a scotch rocks in her right, smoking and sipping in the slow silence. Her pearl-handled Derringer lay in her lap.

When the doorknob rattled to his touch, Mother simply sat, smoked, sipped, inhaled. When the slat of light from the porch fell across the room she exhaled.

He flipped on the study light, jumped, and uttered, "Sheee-it."

Mother drew on her Virginia Slim, blew a cool plume of smoke. "Will, darling." Pause. "This is the new me." Pause. "Like it?" Such timing would be a thing of beauty if not for the circumstances.

That man regrouped quicker than any man I have ever encountered. "Mmmm, baby," he said, all the while unsnapping that hideous pink cowboy shirt with the embroidered yellow lassoes he is so fond of. "That is hot. You kind of look like a soul sister."

"Good," Mother said. "Because if you didn't like it I was reconciled to the idea of putting a bullet into my feeble brain." She picked up the pistol with a dainty little flourish. "Here, sexy. Do something with this instrument of death."

He took the gun, steady slurping at her neck while my lunch wanted to be upchucked. Of course, I might as well have been invisible, and he kept on lapping at her like a horny mutt, talking about how he always wanted a taste of dark meat.

"Ooooh, darling," Mimi squealed. "You know that makes me want to give in to wild abandon. It's absolutely criminal!"

He grunted. He still had not acknowledged me, you will note, intent as he was upon whipping my elderly mother into a hedonistic frenzy. Well, she went into a frenzy all right, and she shared it with the town of Pollard. While that skanky man licked her neck like it was the last lollipop on the planet, she called the police. As was the routine, an officer—this night it was Paul Baggett—let himself in with the spare key Mother had given the department to keep in their one and only squad car. Baggett just stood there, smirking; I was overcome by a paralysis of shame.

Mother stood and swept an accusing arm at Will Luckie, who was mixing himself a fruity gin drink at the bar. "Officer," she panted, "arrest this man!"

Will laughed. I felt defeated.

"Arrest this man on the grounds that he's too goddamned sexy!"

Paul Baggett, too, began to chuckle, licking his chops, I am certain, at the prospect of playing barbershop troubadour the next day.

"Oh, you think I am funning with you?" Ice cubes clinked reiteration in mother's favorite scotch glass. "Well, if you don't arrest this man immediately, I am going to have to tear off my clothes and make love to him with the ardent fervor of a sixteen year-old. And God help your conscience if I have a stroke from it."

Paul Baggett ended up having a beer with them. I went home to Winston.

Sometimes it occurs to me that my daddy died of gallstones and Will Luckie is full of gall. My daddy smoked expensive Cuban cigars and Will Luckie spits. They are day and night. My daddy was a gentleman, even if he wasn't faithful and got drunk a lot. He took care of us. And you know, my DD always told me I would never have to work, that the money would take me into old age, a plush casket, and a choice plot overlooking the Escambia River, with plenty left over for a dozen children. Of course, here I am, childless, because Winston has such difficulty with The Act that we've taken to separate bedrooms over the years, making blundering attempts only when he's had enough merlot, which is difficult for a teetotaler. And Daddy certainly never figured on mother having a geriatric sex-fest with a redneck cowboy swinger who is as low-down as gulley dirt, talks to chickens, and has his eye and his fist on my inheritance.

Oh, Lord, the chickens. I *must* tell you about the chickens. They were the deserving objects of my rage after Will placed the absolute last straw across my load-weary back. He brought three hens and a rooster when he moved in with Mother last fall, then had the nerve to convert the gardener's shed—which sits near my own yard—into a chicken coop. It sends that fecal chicken yard odor across both our back lawns, not to mention the pre-dawn rooster wails and non-stop clucking and flapping. The half-assed fence he put up routinely fails to contain them at all times, so they end up wandering over to the pool and even into Mother's kitchen just last month. Of course you know what Will Luckie did, and Mother and Lindia, for that matter. They laughed. Here you have a yard hen, filthy, full of parasites and histoplasmosis, meandering about the place where food is prepared, and those fools thought it was just about the most humorous occurrence of the decade. I spent the evening Cloroxing Mother's kitchen floor, an already festering incubus of resentment building toward those damned birds, that multiply worse than rabbits.

You see, he has kept on adding more of the feathered beasts throughout the months of his cohabitation with Mother. A few more pullets, another rooster, a couple of Dominekkers, all slick-feathered in rust and green, and then the guineas that got into my winter garden and landed us all in court (the judge, of course, who was utterly taken in, would allow me to sue neither Will nor the guineas). He even bought Mother a peacock, which she adores because it is so flamboyant, like her. It is even named for her—Maureen. Will Luckie named it, of course. He said he could justify using her name because it fit in with the whole Watergate setting of the chicken yard. Oh, did I forget to mention that he put a sign on the chicken coop that said "Watergate Hotel" and named each chicken after that whole Nixon bunch? And with no regard whatsoever to gender. Well that is precisely what the no-count fool did. It started out as a cynical joke, as Will Luckie makes no secret of the fact that he believes he fought in a great big con job (i.e., Vietnam) and spends a great deal of time belittling Republican politicians (of course, my DD is turning in the grave in a whirlwind of cremated ashes at the prospect of Mother copulating with anything resembling a Democrat). But the chicken project took on a deeper meaning for him when he began keeping a daily log, entitled "The Chicken Sheet," in which he records each bird's name, egg production, idiosyncrasies and infirmities. The shell-shocked buffoon began to see the ornithological specimens in a new light; they took on the personality traits characteristic of *homo sapiens* in his deranged mind.

"Martha Mitchell looks peaked today," he writes in the log, or "G. Gordon has been spurring Haldeman all afternoon. Haldeman won't even look him in the eye," or "Erlichman is starting to realize he don't carry no weight in this chicken yard—he has been trying to show out but everybody else ignores him," or "McGruder—three eggs but not a lot of enthusiasm—maybe constipated?" and on and on. It is the only thing near a job I ever witnessed him doing, so you can see right there how useless and sorry that man is. And I am here to tell you he takes that job seriously. J. Dean, Erlichman, J. Mitchell, Seccord, E.H. Hunt—these are their names. There is even an Egil Krogh, which he spells E-a-g-l-e C-r-o-w. And the fastidious detail that goes into the recording of the daily lives of the yard fowl is quite disturbing. He acts as if they've evolved beyond pet-dom, as if they are his bosom buddies, chatting with them as he inventories the nests, caressing that nasty, slimy-looking plumage. Chuck Colson grew so tame from the attention that he let Will Luckie loop a chain dangling a diminutive gold crucifix about his gullet, which he wore for the past month. But it gets even more insane. Just a few days ago, Staff Sergeant Luckie added a bit of green cloth to the chain. He then pinned to the cloth some kind of ridiculous war medal he supposedly earned, making that absurd chicken look like the military dictator of the Watergate Hen House. I swear, I sometimes think that his tours of duty in the jungles of Southeast Asia effectively booby-trapped his little birdbrain.

When a raccoon got into the shed last month and assassinated Tricky-D, that inbred idiot actually got teary-eyed and planned a funeral for the mangled carcass. Then insisted that the family attend. He strummed his guitar and sang "Amazing Grace," all weepy-like. I had not known until that incident just how attached to the poultry he had become. This display of emotion was far and away different from his randy romancing of my aged mother. And this realization of mine undoubtedly saved Will Luckie's life this morning. Let me tell you how it all unfolded:

Winston said he had to stay at the hospital to deliver a baby, so I took a knockout pill and went on to bed, hoping to numb myself with sleep. Sometime before midnight, however, I was awakened by the horrific screams of one who was surely being murdered very, very slowly. When finally, through a fog of cabernet and valium, it dawned upon me that the peacock, Maureen, was the source of the utterances, I was quite relieved, yet could not go back to sleep with those howls punctuating the night. I made my way down to the kitchen and out the back door, which had been left standing wide open. Of course, I assumed that Winston had come in and was reassured by his Cadillac parked in the driveway. But something felt odd; the night seemed a trifle off center, and the scuffling sound coming from around the chicken coop, accompanied by an occasional peacock shriek, drew me to take a silent stroll that would be the terrible undoing of all to which I have grown accustomed.

This is so very difficult, putting into words what I saw there in the moonlight that glowed through the gauze of leaves above. Those garlands of gold (some purchased by my own mother), the ones that were always nestled in the chest curls of Will Luckie, caught the cast of the full moon. He leaned against the outer wall of the old gardener's shed, his breathing filled every few moments with a purring moan, fingers playing across that military-hardened stomach of his. He was caught up in the most intense display of sexual pleasure I have ever witnessed, and I have to confess that some of that pleasure spilled into my own psyche. I felt a mesmerized longing, a huge gulp of desire such as I have never known, until it dawned on me that my own husband was the source of Will Luckie's pleasure.

I have told you about our conjugal difficulties, so it was outside of my frame of reference to see Winston, kneeling there, so caught up in such a perverted act, so absorbed by what he was doing, so oblivious to his surroundings, emitting muffled groans quite unlike the twitters of counterfeit passion he has offered me over the years. I could not move until the lunar light revealed Will Luckie's gaze upon me. And he—you will not begin to believe this, I know—he actually grinned, raised his right hand, extended his index finger, and crooked it at me three times. Can you imagine? Here he is being carnally devoured by my husband, and he has the egomaniacal nerve to invite me to the party! Have you ever in all your life?

The strangest part of this perverse scenario, and I can barely admit it to myself, is that I came within a hair's breadth of walking over, surrendering to God knows what. It was hypnotic, and the stirrings within me were so white-hot and demanding. All I knew was a feverish desperation for some implied promise of satisfaction, something I know very little of, unfortunately; but, just as I started forward, Will Luckie let out a gasping moan that sent me headlong toward the sensuous safety of my own bedroom.

Needless to say, I did not sleep at all that night. My bewildered arousal and shock gave way to a mulling inventory of the scores of wrongs done unto me until, as dawn broke, I found myself in the throes of a righteous rage that wanted only to be visited upon Will Luckie. That is when I made my way to Mother's garage and loaded my DD's shotgun.

I paused at the door to the study, where Mother's man-whore had apparently passed out, and contemplated his murder. There is no doubt that I will roast in hellfire for all

126

eternity behind the homicidal inklings that rustled about my brain, but at this point I fail to give a shit. You see, when earthly anguish (as in the form of one's lunatic mother, her sexually ambiguous leech of a boyfriend, and my cheating impostor of a husband) becomes infused within the pores of one's flesh so that Lucifer's den looks to be a relief, then the time to act has arrived. And so I acted. And I did Will Luckie one better.

I acted upon those goddamned yard birds of his. Chuck Colson met me at the gate, having been taught to hold high expectations of those humans who serve him. I laid the stock on my hip, got my palm beneath the barrel, and fired, silently thanking my DD for teaching me to shoot. It struck me that a shotgun went a long way toward decimating coop fowl, effectively blowing them to smithereens, as it were. You have never seen such a tornado of feathers in your life, a maelstrom of beaks, guts, gristle and feet. A few wings in the throes of dancing nerves, jitterbugging against dirt-grained blood in the chicken yard, slinging dots of bright red against the shed. I managed to annihilate Erlichman, Seccord, Krogh, and Liddy before folks came running. I accidentally fired into the bay window in Mother's kitchen trying to hit Martha Mitchell, who had flapped over to the patio thinking I would not notice her there, trying to blend in with the potted white begonias, and the sound of breaking glass tinkled like wind chimes into the hurricane of squawks, screeches and stacattoing wings on Mother's dewey green lawn. I got John Dean and Haldeman, vaguely aware of Will Luckie's stream of curses, his moan of anguish as he raked through meaty feathers for his Bronze Star and crucifix, a moan quite distinct from the orgasmic howl of the previous midnight. My mother's profane shrieks of hysteria against the tableau of sounds grated against my very last nerve and I admit to a flash of a desire to turn the gun on her. That was when Angus Stevens from across the street wrestled my DD's gun away from me. Of course the P.C.P.D. was absolutely thrilled to wheel up to a real emergency—a bona fide chicken massacre—at Miss Maureen's.

Mother was in her vicious-tongued mode. "CeCe, you have lost every bit of your goddamn mind!" she screamed, as down snowflaked upon the wig she still wore behind the hair burning. "Is this what you foresaw when you gave your heart to Jesus? Murdering sweet creatures that give us our morning nourishment?"

"Oh, the humanity!" Officer Baggett murmured.

"If you had only lived life a little, you would not be capable of such cold, lunatic rage!" Mother went on. "And didn't I always try to get you to live a goddamn life? Didn't I?" She quieted a moment and actually took a deep breath. "If you could only learn to live and laugh. Laugh at yourself. Laugh at this absurd life! Then you could never be so vicious as to murder poor Will's friends. You have no idea what you have done to him. Goddamn, I need a Bloody-fucking-Mary."

Of course, I did not argue with her, not in front of the police and the neighbors. It would only encourage her to provide more raw drama for the townspeople to view. And I certainly did not tell her about Winston and Will Luckie. I can never do that! Lord, what would folks think of me then? I do not believe there has ever been a homosexual incident in Pollard, and I am not about to go down as a witness to the first homosexual incident on record.

As I climbed into the police car—Baggett insisted that I sit up front with him—I spied Will Luckie by the pool. He had that little net he uses to clean leaves and bugs out of the chlorined water, but on this landmark morning he was dipping at some of the feathers, still drifting on currents of air like ashes from a barrel burning, or a cremation, that had landed in the pool. His shoulders were hunched over, shaking. It was obvious that he was sobbing as he dipped the remnants of the Watergate conspirators out of the cold liquid. I was able to take a little satisfaction in that. Hell, he is probably having a huge funeral for them as we speak. I wouldn't be surprised if he purchased marble slabs and headstones with more of my inheritance money—created a memorial garden for the Watergate gang, with an air-conditioned vault for Chuck's remains, of course.

So here I am. Mother is not pressing charges, of course, but James Caffey, her attorney, says that the state might have to, because firing into a residence is a felony. I imagine that Mr. Caffey is working on bailing me out right this minute.

I suppose jail is quite reprehensible in a bigger town than Pollard, but here it is quite homey. Baggett, Trent Givens, and Rita, that sweet little dispatcher who does the wake-up call service, brought me lunch from the Jitney Jungle, let me use the phone to cancel the Ladies' Club meeting this evening, and they even rolled a TV into my cell so I could watch the Watergate hearings. That John Dean is testifying. He is kind of a squirrely little man, but have you seen his wife? Maureen? She is gorgeous, not a blonde hair out of place. Perfect skin. Big eyes and big earbobs. She has style. Even a stylish nickname—"Mo." I almost feel bad about shooting her husband.

I must insist upon one thing. You cannot tell a soul about Winston's indiscretion. Surely I can trust you folks. Surely I have nothing to worry about where you all are concerned. Hell, we don't even know any of the same people I'll bet. I mean you two are from Pensacola, right? And you are in for assault? No, I am certain we could not know the same people. Moreover, we understand our status, one to the other. Status is tres important, a thing worth fighting for, a thing worth preserving. You know, after lo these many months of Will Luckie's ill-mannered, low-life ways, it is a relief to have this sense of clarity about the state of us, don't you think?

The Seamstress

"Well, all I can say about that," Mrs. Clark Hogan Wilson pronounced, with the bearing of a robed, gaveled judge, and even more of the authority, "is that Sarah Jo Cooper never had any inkling about how to keep herself a cut above the riff-raff."

Mrs. Wilson, "Francie" to her most bosom of friends, lifted a dimpled little hand to brush a puff of parlor-dyed curls back from her forehead, revealing grooved wrinkles born of brow-knitting and, on a typical day, glaring as she sulked. Today, however, she was not sulking, riding instead the crest of an exhilarating wave of self-importance while she engaged in the gossip that nourished her. She stood on a four-by-four raised platform, feeling that much higher than her handmaidens, while a seamstress altered the ball gown she was to wear a week from Friday.

She had just been regaled with the tale of Sarah Jo Cooper, who had left her husband of thirty-two years to ride off into the sunset with a drywall hanger who was renovating the antebellum home said husband had bought for her only a month prior. "Once trash, always trash," Mrs. Wilson said. "I believe I pointed that out to you at Mitzi Stanton's last dinner party if you'll recall. Do you recall that? Do you?"

"I most certainly do," her most recent best friend Camilla, Mrs. James Cunningham Dixon, replied, as the seamstress worked at pinning Mrs. Wilson's hem.

The seamstress, Celeste, had observed this cannibalistic friendship over the previous weeks of fittings and alterations as she constructed Mrs. Wilson's Mardi Gras gown. She had noted that Mrs. Dixon was tenacious about doing her duty as a hanger-on, bearing platters of giddy gossip for her mentor to consume. Gifted with an encyclopedic knowledge of maiden names and double first cousins, Mrs. Dixon could sniff out vague ancestral connections to any scandal and find genealogical secrets that would horrify the sensibility of a St. Louis streetwalker. She had even prodded Celeste, a deliberately private soul, for personal information, for a family history from which to gain a point of reference. She had been delighted when she discovered that Celeste had grown up with her own maternal third cousin, Martha Sams, in Brannon, Mississippi, south and west of Columbus, immediately seeing that cousin Martha could offer the lowdown on Celeste.

In addition to her role as Troubador of Troubles, Purveyor of Peccadilloes, Mrs. Dixon also undertook her task of Flatterer-in-Chief to Mrs. Wilson with an effusive fervor. "You are an excellent judge of character, Francie. It's pure power of perception. You simply *know* people through and through, and I do recall that you pointed that out to me about Sarah Jo Cooper. Saw right clear through her. I swear, you don't miss a beat," she gushed.

Mrs. Wilson picked a piece of lint from the velvet skirt of her gown and flicked it into the air. It dipped and danced like dwarfed confetti. "Of course you also recall that it was at Mitzi's tacky little dinner party," she said. "Do you recall that embarrassing nightmare of a party?"

"Absolutely do," Mrs. Dixon said. "It was right there at that selfsame party that you pointed out to me about Sarah Jo's flawed character. You pointed out to me how cozy she was with the help. How she had her head leaned in to that college boy bartender who—"

"The one in the tiki hut," Mrs. Wilson said. "Do you recall that tacky little tiki hut Mitzi had set up by the pool as an island bar?"

"Well of course. How could I not? It was the one with the young college boy bartending in it. A medical student, I think."

"It was a Hawaiian luau theme you see, Celeste. A luau is a Hawaiian feast, did you know?" Mrs. Wilson spoke down to the woman at her feet. "All of our parties—well, the very best ones, anyway—they all have a theme. You know, the creation of a tableau, a setting, a dramatic flair."

"My, how elegant." Celeste, the seamstress, pulled another straight pin from her wrist cushion, working with the gold net material bunched at Mrs. Wilson's waist, draped down around the rich, deep purple velvet gown, the tips of her nimble fingers faintly aware of little sausage-like rolls of fatty flesh beneath the clingy fabric. "Now, Mrs. Wilson, it's important that you bring those shoes you plan to wear with this when you come for your next fitting. This netting is very tricky to hem and—"

"Yes yes yes," Mrs. Wilson said in her hurried, impatient voice. "But as I was saying just now, the theme is what makes the party, if you have the flair to make it work. Believe you me, there is nothing more pitiful than a flopped theme."

"Well you wouldn't know about that, Francie," Mrs. Dixon said, rummaging through an oversized handbag. "I'm telling you, Celeste, there is nothing like one of Francie's parties. They are the best, bar none. You should get to see one before you die, my hand to God. Do you want a Life Saver?" she held out the roll of candy, its foil wrapper peeled and hanging like tossed serpentine.

"No, thank you," Celeste said. The gold netting was stiff and unwieldy next to the supple purple velvet. "Would you lift your arm, please?"

Mrs. Wilson complied, sending the sprung flesh on the underside of her arm into a series of jiggles. "Like last August. I had an all black party last August. Not black *people*, you know, but a black décor, like a wake or a funeral, for Hogie's fiftieth birthday party. And he's way older than me, so don't you even think it. Do you recall that party, Camilla?"

"It was only the be-all end-all of birthday parties," Camilla gushed. Celeste pulled another straight pin from the red satin wrist cushion. Her own husband had not seen fifty, had died instead, at twenty-eight, leaving her with four small children, a Singer sewing machine, and an avalanche of debt, estranged from the family that could have helped her.

"And the all black party was such a hit that on New Year's I had an all white party, just like those jet setter folks do. You know, everything white—white food, like sour cream and cream cheese dips, and vanilla cakes and this divine, frothy white wine punch. Oh—and white flowers. You know, floating camellias and such. And white candles—white everything."

"It was nothing short of fabulous, Celeste," Mrs. Dixon, ever the sycophant, effused. "Francie throws the best parties of anyone in our circle, and you don't even get into our circle unless you know how to throw a grand party. Well, except for Mitzi Stanton, I guess."

"*Our* circle?" Mrs. Wilson lifted one eyebrow with arch indictment and let it soak in for a moment. Then she smiled with forced benevolence. "At any rate, it is no small feat to be a successful hostess, I am here to tell you. It takes quite a lot of thought and creativity. You can't believe all the little details you have to be mindful of. Just one tiny thing can cause a huge flop."

"My," Celeste said again.

"Right down to the guests," Mrs. Wilson went on. "You have to take care to have a complementary mix of temperaments and a code of dress. Of course, the guests at my white party were all required to wear white, so as not to disturb the theme. You have to be very specific on what to wear. Some people just don't have any finesse. Lord, my arm is tired. Can't I put it down?"

"Yes, ma'am." Celeste drew back and studied the netting she was attempting to drape as per instructions from Mrs. Wilson, who continued her pontification on the art of hostessing a successful party.

"If just one guest breaks the dress code, well, it simply sticks out like a sore thumb. It ruins the larger picture—the canvas, if you will. Anyway, I imagine I have just about done it all, party theme-wise."

"But whenever we think she's outdone herself, she comes up with a brand new twist. It's a flair, that's all. It's an inborn talent." Mrs. Dixon took a compact out of her purse and powdered down her nose. "I declare, I shine like a lighthouse beacon. And I don't have the first idea how to have my hair done for the ball." She scrutinized the stiffly layered flaps of frosty blonde, turning her head at sharp angles. "Good night alive, these highlights are all wrong."

Mrs. Dixon was in the process of moving from a social stratum just beneath that of Mrs. Wilson and into the one Mrs. Wilson presided over, so well done highlights were of utmost importance. Mrs. Wilson herself was hoping to be elected president of her Mardi Gras society the next time around, poised to launch up to the next social level, the one that every great once in a while pierced the true aristocracy of coastal Alabama.

Mrs. Dixon snapped the compact shut. "I do know one thing, though. Even a magnificent Mardi Gras ball hasn't got much on one of Francie's parties. Go on, Francie, and try to tell Celeste all the themes you've done just this past year," Mrs. Dixon urged.

"Well, let's see," Mrs. Wilson said. "I've done a Roaring Twenties party and a Screen Siren—that's where you come as a movie star. Hogie and I were Liz and Dick. Anyway, a Screen Siren party, a Beach Blanket Bingo party over the bay, a Monaco Casino party at the country club. Gosh, it must be a half dozen. And I'm here to tell the both of you that a Hawaiian luau with a tiki hut bar, a bunch of plastic leis, and Don Ho ukulele music comes a dime a dozen."

"Isn't that the gospel," Mrs. Dixon chimed in. "It's practically one of the commandments: 'Thou shalt not throw a Hawaiian luau.' But then, Mitzi Stanton has nothing near your sense of style, Francie. On top of that, she's a Jew. I don't think they even believe in the Ten Commandments, do they?"

"Yes," the seamstress said. "They do."

"Anyway, that was just fluff about the commandments," Mrs. Dixon said. "My main point was about Francie having oodles of style and Mitzi having not one blessed drop."

"Well at the risk of seeming big-headed, I certainly won't contradict that," Mrs. Wilson said. "And that is why I was elected parliamentarian and historian of the Merry Makers over Mitzi Stanton. The only reason we let her join in the first place was because her husband is Methodist and the premiere auto salesman in Mobile. A Jew and Mardi Gras is oil and water, so she had no business being an officer. The gall. But after that tacky little luau of hers, she might as well have just put a sign on wheels out front of her house saying, 'Mitzi Stanton has no flair whatsoever'. There was no way she could have avoided me beating her in that election."

"It was a landslide, Celeste," Mrs. Dixon said to the seamstress. "It was practically a unanimous mandate."

"Goodness." Celeste walked a slow circle around Mrs. Wilson, studying the fit of the sequined bodice. Mardi Gras sparkles of purple and gold winked promises from the roly-poly pudge of Mrs. Clark Hogan Wilson.

"Oh, absolutely. A landslide," Mrs. Wilson reiterated. "And an honor, of course. A position of leadership, which is where you ought to be if you have flair and a keen sense of style. I mean, the business of the Merry Makers is to have party after party. Leading up to the big party during Mardi Gras, of course. It takes a keen sense of style."

"Well, honey, that is you. That is just you all over," Mrs. Dixon cooed, retrieving an emery board from the handbag and commencing to sand the edges of her fingernails. "I swanee, my nails look like a scrub woman's." The scritch of the emery board punctuated a short silence before Mrs. Dixon remembered to re-focus on her friend. "Like I say, Francie, style is simply your calling card. You could have stepped right out of *Cosmopolitan* or *Vogue*." She craned her neck to see the seamstress, who again worked on the netting at Mrs. Wilson's back. "I'm sure you know, Celeste, "that Mrs. Wilson will be showcased at the tableau. Which means, of course, that your dressmaking skills will be showcased."

"It's exciting all right," Celeste said. She had been hearing for months about how Mrs. Wilson would be presented as an officer of her Mardi Gras society at a grand processional, or tableau, before the ball. It was a huge event, the penultimate pinnacle of Mrs. Wilson's social history as one who jockeyed for every movement upward she could garner. "I will be proud to have you model my work."

"Oh, but Celeste, sweetie, it's as much how you wear a dress as how it's made," Mrs. Wilson said. "More, even. Let's face it. Anybody and their sister can make a dress. Lord, I bet retards make them in factories all the time. I mean, the real flair is in the wearing of it, don't you think?"

"Yes. Of course." Celeste, practiced in the art of appearing unruffled by insensitivity, began unpinning and re-pinning the gold netting around the back of the dress.

She had tried to tell Mrs. Wilson that the netting would clash with the texture of velvet and had urged her to pick a grainy satin for the skirt of her gown, but Mrs. Wilson would have none of it. Mrs. Wilson had been looking for a specific effect, "a Marie Antoinette effect," she had said, "all swooped out on the sides, you know, but add a part hanging down the back. Almost a train, you know. A French queen for the Mardi Gras ball—*le bon temps*."

French like a New Orleans whore, Celeste had thought.

Mrs. Wilson had been coming to her dressmaking parlor for over twenty years, as had an entire parade of ladies and little girls carrying mounds of satin, Chantilly lace, dotted Swiss, *poi du sois*, crepe, velveteen—fabrics that cocooned their social stations in life like spun silk. She threaded embroidery into fine linen christening gowns, stitched the smocking across toddlers' dresses, sewed red and black velvet cuffs onto tartan plaid Christmas dresses, secured pastel netting over bridesmaids' skirts, and attached mother of pearl beads and Irish lace onto wedding gowns. She ran her tape measure around the busts, waists and hips of the women, down the lengths of their backs, an intimacy ripe with irony. She aided well-dressed ladies in elaborate deceptions, drawing and cutting patterns for designer copies—which was the most lucrative part of the business—and she deposited the women's folded bills and personal checks into her own burgeoning bank account. The stock market investments she made had doubled, tripled, then quadrupled the fees provided by the ladies who commanded her services.

In recent years she had begun to look forward to a very comfortable early retirement. Now, in the midst of her forties, she was finally winding down, putting the last of her children through college, coming upon her own time in life. And she had taken more abuse than she would have ever predicted when she ran away from home at the age of seventeen, from wealthy parents in the Mississippi Black

Belt, just to be with the man who loved her briefly, and very well, indeed, before he died.

A couple of her clients were not just from old, but *very* old, money—Old Mobile aristocrats who would never deign to boast as Mrs. Wilson did, but who held on to a slick, sterling silver barrier of aloofness, a much more subtle, polite kind of reminder that Celeste's purpose in life was to be at their beck and call, which often meant kneeling at their feet. Unlike the social unfoldings of Mrs. Wilson's Mystic Order of Mirthful Merry Makers, their Mardi Gras functions were written up in vast detail in the *Mobile Press Register*. Their King and Queen were treated like the blue-blood royalty they were born to be, their expensive crowns bought and paid for by money seeded by robber barons, then aged in timber, shipping, and double deals. Celeste hated them, save for one or two, with a fierce purity. She hated the low esteem in which she was held by them. And, having refused her own inheritance, having put it aside for her grandchildren, she hated the inherited currency her customers bestowed upon her after she worked on the hems of their garments, bowed there at their feet like a penitent parishioner seeking absolution.

But she hated Mrs. Wilson and her ilk a million times more, hated their hungry grasps at that higher station in life she had shunned, their shallow little battles, the meager stakes they raised above their means. Mrs. Clark Hogan Wilson epitomized it all, and Celeste had watched her for over two decades, coming up a notch or two here, down one notch there, her long, futile climb tearing at what little potential for a soul had ever rested in her heart in the first place.

Mrs. Clark Hogan Wilson talked about the local aristocrats—the Fillinghams, Dolans, McColloughs—as if they were more than passing acquaintances of hers. "Who will be the next Queen of Carnival?" she would ask. "Of course, we knew Maxine Dolan would have it this year, but next year there's going to be a huge battle between Lexus Dolan and that Mary McCollough. Their daddies are likely to come to blows. Isn't it delicious?" Celeste thought this talk of hers analogous to those pathetic women who discussed TV soap opera characters as they would friends or family members, filling their empty lives with the escapades and tribulations of the fictional characters portrayed by third rate stars.

Mr. Clark Hogan Wilson was a merchant who had made it to the top of the floor covering market in town, complete with television commercials on the local stations—"Let Hogie make your home homey," the jingle went—bringing in plenty of money, though never enough, in Mrs. Wilson's eyes, to erase his lack of a college education. As she aged, she shaded the truth about her husband by degree, until he became "an honorary Kappa Sigma at the University," and "an honorary member of the Wolf Landing Hunting Club," and "an influential player in city politics."

No one seemed willing to call her on her lies. Celeste, as always, chose to keep her stoic, perfected silence and her fruitful livelihood, for the sake of her children. Sometimes, though, she felt as if she were treading silent black waters, gasping for air, grappling for a lifeboat captained by Mrs. Wilson, whose history was the antithesis of her own principled past, an impostor of a captain who all the while pushed down on her, shoving her head under the waves, beating her back from the vessel with an oar.

"It will be nothing short of magnificent, Celeste," Mrs. Dixon was saying.

"What is that?" Celeste silently cursed the stiff netting.

"The tableau, of course. The tableau." Mrs. Dixon squirmed and giggled like an antsy kindergartner. "I know it's supposed to be very top secret and all, Francie. And I know it's going to be my first time as a guest at the Mystic Merry Makers' Ball, but can't I please tell Celeste just a little? Just a little about the tableau?"

Celeste pulled another pin from the shiny red satin wrist cushion.

Mrs. Wilson sighed. "Oh, all right. But Celeste had better not go blabbing our secrets to just anybody, because not just anybody gets to come to our ball."

"Celeste won't tell, will you, Celeste?"

"No," the seamstress said.

"All right, then." She set her handbag on the floor and sat up very straight. "First of all, there will be the most elaborate costumes you can imagine. All two hundred and forty members will be in the processional. Their husbands will be seated along the edges of the arena, wearing dignified tuxedos, of course. And the members will wear these gorgeous costumes. But naturally you know they are gorgeous, because you made lots of them yourself."

"Yes, I did," said the seamstress.

"Anyway, the theme this year is 'Let the Good Times Roll All Around the World,' so each group of ten or twelve ladies will be dressed in costumes native to a particular country. And they'll do a dance to some taped music—related to that country, you know. And this will go on and on and on. Until the big moment."

Celeste fingered a sequin that had snagged loose from the bodice. "I'll have to fix this," she murmured.

"The big moment is when they introduce the five officers, one by one. And these spotlights follow them down from the stage and across the arena. And they do a Mardi Gras dance to some New Orleans jazz and the president introduces the queen and the queen commands the ball to begin and oh, I am so excited!"

"My goodness, Camilla, get a Xanax out of my purse and calm yourself," Mrs. Wilson said. "But I admit it will be a thrill to be followed across an arena by spotlights while hundreds of people seated in the audience watch. Kind of like being Miss America. And to think it might have been that Jewess Mitzi Stanton instead of me, if not for that tacky Hawaiian luau she threw. Goodness, I'm tired of standing on this step-stool."

"You can get dressed now," Celeste said. "I think I see what needs to be done."

Mrs. Dixon babbled on and on about the tableau while Mrs. Wilson changed clothes. "I mean, I've been to balls before, and they were nice. But this is the Mystic Order of Mirthful Merry Makers. They are known to have the best ball, besides the top two societies, of course. And you have to practically marry into those, you know."

Celeste almost said, "Yes, I know about marrying into even more money, because that is what my father expected, only I chose not to take my father's fortune and double it by merging assets with another family. I did not prostitute myself to a man I did not love." She often wanted to spit the truth at them, tell them what a sham it all was, their desperate bid for upward mobility. "When you marry for money, you earn every penny," her husband used to say, and Celeste knew that these women could have only reached their desired level by marrying into it, and they had certainly not done that. Too, marrying up would have been a long shot, at best, for women like them, shallow and unbeautiful as they were. No, the heart pine core of aristocracy they lusted after was a closed society, and they would never be allowed into the club. Not that club, the one in which she had been reared. Never that ultimate club.

Mrs. Dixon caught Celeste's gaze, pointed at a scrap of the gold netting on the floor, and mouthed the words, enough of a whisper that Celeste could hear her. "That just does not go," she whispered, shaking her head, wide-eyed.

Celeste shrugged.

"Remember to bring your shoes to your next fitting," Celeste said again, when Mrs. Wilson emerged from the hallway that served as a makeshift dressing room.

"Yes, I know. I don't have to be told a thing forty times," Mrs. Wilson huffed, rolling her eyes at her friend.

"Oh, Celeste," Mrs. Dixon said. "My cousin Martha is coming down from Brannon to visit this weekend. I'll tell her hello for you."

"Yes. Do that," the seamstress said.

"And I warn you, Miss Mysterious. My cousin Martha will give me the scoop on you and yours. So if you have some big old juicy secrets, well—look out."

"I certainly will," the seamstress said. "Goodness."

"I know what, Francie. You must do the dance," Mrs. Dixon said. "Before we go, you must do the dance for Celeste."

"Yes, our little Cinderella. Our poor little Cinderella who needs a fairy godmother to transform her for the ball," Mrs. Wilson said.

Celeste gathered the cast off gown into her arms, gold netting stiff and scratchy. "What sort of dance?"

"The Mardi Gras dance. You know the one. Like this." Mrs. Wilson began to strut, the familiar Mardi Gras strut so common on the streets of New Orleans and Mobile. "Da-da-*da*," she sang, dipping and swaying. "Da-da-*dadada*. Da-da-*da*. Da-da-*dadada*. And here comes the good part." She did a half turn and broke into a backward strut while Mrs. Dixon joined her in the song. And they both danced their way out the front door, laughing a rowdy chorus of anticipation while the seamstress pressed the crisp gold netting to her cheek and contemplated their reverie.

When Mrs. Wilson returned the following week for her final fitting, gold shoes in hand, she was sans her usual appendage, the fawning Mrs. Dixon. She was also oddly quiet, the sulk lines in her forehead grooved in a fixed petulance as she stood on the small platform. Celeste re-pinned the hem and double-checked each seam, the zipper, the hook and eye, the malignant gold netting all webbed out like a cancer around the skirt. The room was a jumble of sparkling gold, yellow, green, purple—fluffs of flounces, bolts of beaded and brocade fabrics for the Carnival season. Last minute gowns lay about in various stages of glitter, some gaudily playful with festive flashes of rhinestones, others like garish Las Vegas neon, ready to play out to a night all boozy and sour with stomach-turning dances and sloppy, slathered-on kisses from strangers.

"You don't wear your gown on the float, do you?" Celeste asked. "It could be a problem getting—"

"Well of course not," Mrs. Wilson snapped, breaking her silence in two. "Don't you know anything? We have to wear masks and costumes that go with the theme of the float. My God. Why would you even *have* a float if you weren't going to have costumes? Just why?"

Celeste tugged at the sequined shoulder strap. Mrs. Wilson's flaccid skin pooched around it; more flesh spilled in a bratwurst-like bulge over the top of the scoop-necked back. "This seems fine," the seamstress said.

"I'll tell you what *seems*," Mrs. Wilson snapped again. "It *seems* to me that you often ignore what I say. It seems to me that you often behave rudely. Like now. You do not show one bit of interest in the workings of the float."

"I never cared much for Mardi Gras parades. I only went when my children were small." Celeste made gentle rearrangements in the gold netting that swept around the sides of the velvet skirt.

"And I admit I don't care much for the parades, either, so don't think you're anything special," Mrs. Wilson said. Her voice had an angry, tense tone that Celeste had not heard before. "I don't want to be gobbed up in those hordes of people on the sidewalk, that's for sure. The unwashed masses." She shuddered. "I'm telling you, you get a birds' eye view of the dregs of Mobile from high up on a float."

Celeste uttered her favorite of her standard remarks. "Goodness."

"You can't tell me you wouldn't like to be a float rider. You can't tell me you wouldn't like folks to be yelling to you for beads or moon pies. It's like being a queen. It's like being Cleopatra coming down the Nile on a gilded barge. I don't understand anybody that wouldn't like that."

Celeste moved to the other side of Mrs. Wilson's skirt, to the other pouf of gold.

"No, I don't understand it one little bit," Mrs. Wilson went on. "Oh, I'm sure plenty of folks would *say* they didn't want to be a float rider, but those are the ones that are so jealous they wouldn't ever admit how much they deep down want to take your place. But I can't for the life of me understand somebody that gets to be a float rider and then walks away from it like it's nothing. Like it's not worth a damn thing. Do you understand somebody like that?"

"Well, I suppose it's—"

"Somebody like that is just mean or crazy or stupid is what I think. Somebody like that maybe has brain cancer or some kind of schizophrenia to walk away from what counts."

Celeste knelt at Mrs. Wilson's back, checking the hem of the faux train, seeing how it lined up with the glittering three-inch heels she wore.

"It's a disgrace is what." Mrs. Wilson huffed and blew like a spooked pony. "It makes me want to spit to high heaven."

Celeste stood. "I'll send this over to Lawson's Dry Cleaning to have it pressed for you as soon as I get it hemmed. You can pick it up there on Thursday."

"You do that," Mrs. Wilson said in a voice thick with sarcasm. She stepped down, wobbling on her heels. Celeste caught her elbow, but the other woman jerked it away and stomped off to the hallway dressing room.

"I guess you see that Camilla Dixon, my little pilot fish, is no longer at my side," Mrs. Wilson, still boiling, shouted from the hallway. "She's like to have a breakdown, too, because I have officially uninvited her to the Merry Makers' Ball. As an officer I am allowed to do that. You see?"

"Oh?"

"Some people just don't know when to shut up. Some people say more than anybody wants to know, that's all."

"Yes. They do," the seamstress said.

"But not you. No. Never you. You don't do a damn thing to let on what cards you've been dealt, do you? You keep your trump hand right up against your chest, don't you?"

Celeste smiled. "I don't play cards."

Mrs. Wilson burst through the door, flushed and trembling. She flung the dress across the room. "See that you get this finished right away," she commanded.

"Of course," the seamstress said.

Mrs. Wilson snatched several bills from her purse. "I have your money. And, oh—here's something else." She dug down into her handbag, coming out with a handful of throws. "Since you won't be at the parade," she said, and threw beads, bills, doubloons, and a lone moon pie across the room, the dinging and clattering of the cheap trinkets like a percussive curse against the hardwood floor.

Celeste watched her priss her chubby frame through the front door, where she turned and scowled her best, deepest-wrinkled sneer at the seamstress. "Camilla was right about one thing, though."

"Really?"

"Yes. Really. She was right about how you ought to experience at least one of my parties. Maybe you could serve *hors d'oeuvres* for me sometime, or pop out of a cake or something equally cheap, like what you have chosen in life."

"Oh, I don't know," Celeste said. "I'm really only good at sewing. That, I am quite good at. But you might consider asking my son, Hollis. He does a little private bartending to help with college expenses."

"Is that so? Well, I'm sure I am honored that you chose to reveal something about your personal life to little old me. A son. And in college, no less."

"Just finishing medical school," Celeste said. "But he won't be available much longer. He'll be doing his internship. And he's engaged, too. A very nice girl, very down to earth. Mary McCollough."

For a split second it seemed to Celeste that Mrs. Wilson's sneer would be wiped away by utter shock, but it held steady, set there in the grooves of her face, her eyes ripe with pure hatred.

"You go to your choosing and rot like a trashy beggar in hell," Mrs. Wilson said, slamming the door hard enough to rattle windowpanes in the adjoining room.

Celeste retrieved the throws and the cash, then picked up the mangled purple velvet with its clashing Marie Antoinette gold netting. She walked over to her time-worn Singer sewing machine, spread the skirt back and out, and then set to work on the hem, the stabbing and clicketing of the piston-borne needle sealing her resolve.

The Mardi Gras season came to a drunken climax on Fat Tuesday and faded into the confessions of a hungover Ash Wednesday, and the ladies who came into Celeste's place of business were abuzz with the tales of intrigue, subterfuge, strife, and backbiting that so often accompanies large-scale social gatherings.

But by far the most buzzed about tale was that of the bizarre and shocking occurrences at the Mystic Order of Mirthful Merry Makers' events. All along the parade route, it was told, Mrs. Clark Hogan Wilson would go missing for an inordinate while, only to be found in the Port-o-Potty hidden in the bowels of the float, miserably shoveling moon pie after moon pie into her jowly little face, eyes glazed over in a sugary chocolate-induced haze. She would be brought up to her place high at the top of the float, a facsimile of a pink Matterhorn with purple clouds towering above the crush of the crowd, above the minions who were corralled back like sheep by grilled metal barricades. She would throw a few handfuls from the large box hidden behind a cliff in the Matterhorn, then, when no one was noticing, would make her way again to the Port-o-Potty, another stash of chocolate moon pies hidden deep in her bra and in the folds of her emerald green satin Swiss Alps costume.

Mrs. Wilson's mood picked up later, most agreed, as the members of the Mystic Order of Mirthful Merry Makers retired to the Civic Center to prepare for their tableau. Everyone agreed it was a beautiful tableau this year, maybe even better than any society in town. The China Dolls, Flamenco Dancers, Hula Girls, Belly Dancers—group after group, they waltzed, twirled and waddled their way across the arena to the applause of the crowd, the ceremonial flash and swoop of spotlights, the twinkling of sequins on satin.

Then the arena fell silent as the officers, in various states of elegance and pre-eminence, took the stage. Mrs. Wilson was announced first, illuminated by three white lights that tossed the glitter of her sequined bodice out to the audience as she began her walk down the stairs to the Mardi Gras song. The three spotlights brushed her round frame, the deep purple velvet skirt netted over by gold. When she reached the arena floor, she broke into the traditional strut while the onlookers clapped hands to the rhythm.

And it was told all over town what happened when she turned to execute her signature flair, to strut her backward strut. It seemed, they said, to happen in slow motion, that the heel of one gold shoe caught in the netting, and, in that instant, all that followed became inevitable. Her arms flailed, the crowd sucked in a collective gale of a gasp, the other foot stepped back, even farther into the netting, pulling the first shoe completely off, and pulling her the rest of the way down. She tumbled to her ample buttocks with a padded thud, sitting in the middle of the arena floor, legs outspread, all dignity seared away. Even worse, the jolting force of her landing, it seemed, had liberated one lone moon pie from the brassiere prison where it had resided since her chocolate binge on the Merry Makers' float. The chocolate covered disc of cake and marshmallow hit the floor beside her, cellophane glinting as it spun in the Miss America spotlight. And it did a twirling little dance of its own before coming to a rest on the waxed floor of the arena next to her cast off shoe.

From the hushed audience came a twitter or two, but these were hurriedly shushed by others, who then twittered a bit themselves. A long forever of stunned silence passed before a couple of the tuxedoed men—not her husband, who was frozen with embarrassed horror—leapt to their feet to help her up. One of them gallantly and discretely pocketed the moon pie in an effort to restore a fraction of dignity to the occasion. Then, like an awkward Prince Charming, he bent down to hold the sparkly gold shoe as she wiggled and worked her plump foot into it.

Of course, the music swelled again, and the processional went on. The other officers were introduced, and the president introduced the queen, and the queen commanded that the ball begin. And, after crying on the shoulders of her most bosom of friends, Mrs. Clark Hogan Wilson danced all evening with a smile fixed to her face, fixed like the grin of a stalked and trophied animal from a taxidermy establishment, attempting to make light of the ruination of her vertical advancement.

Efforts to put a gag order into effect for the members of the Mystic Order of Mirthful Merry Makers were futile, and the events of that evening were carried from function to function by wagging tongues, received with doubled-over laughter, and passed on. The story was unstoppable, and it grew exponentially, on its inevitable course of becoming a Mardi Gras Legend. The moon pie, too, became an icon, was auctioned off at charity events, passed from Mardi Gras society to Mardi Gras society and beyond, along with the tale of Mrs. Clark Hogan Wilson.

And the tale was told again and again, at bridge clubs and teas, in nail salons, beauty parlors, and shops. It was told at the country clubs of the nearly elite and at the exclusive clubs of the most elite. And it was told in the fitting room of the seamstress, Celeste, who knelt at the feet of the ladies, working the fine fabrics of their choosing. It was told over and over, while the seamstress, she with the most vindicated of hearts, turned bland bolts of material into crisp summer blouses edged in navy blue piping and full, cinch-waisted skirts swirling the colors of stained glass windows between her practiced and nimble fingers.

All the Way to Memphis

"The truth does not change according to our ability to stomach it."
—Flannery O'Connor

Clista Juniper was a meticulous woman, from her immaculate housekeeping to her perfectly enunciated sentences; from the way she comported herself with pitch-perfect professionalism to the way she presided over the Hinds County High library. The school was situated between the county seat of Jackson, Mississippi, and Raymond, which was known as "the other county seat," a fact that amused her with its ironical aberration, its lack of order. It even extended to her daily wardrobe, which consisted of tailored suits in every shade of beige so that the coral lips and nails, with matching pumps, her trademark, would stand out all the more, her platinum-dyed hair double-French twisted in a tight, inwardly curling labial sheen, a la Tippi Hedren. Indeed, her colleagues—for she had no real intimates—often teased her about her early sixties look, whereupon Clista might express her practiced, breathy giggle and respond, "It is me, the look. Always has been."

"Right down to the girdle?" a teacher might ask.

"Absolutely."

"With the clips and all?" another might chime in.

"Certainly."

"They still make those?"

"I have always believed in stocking up."

"What's a girdle?" a neophyte, a young woman poorly read who took no note of puns, might ask.

So Clista, though she was senior staff at sixty-something, would leave it to another woman, a fifty-something, to explain, getting back to her shelves and her silence and her computerized Dewey Decimal System (although she maintained a card catalogue as well), shushing students with a coral pucker against her coral-nailed index finger.

The automobile she was driving on this day, her champagne-colored Cadillac, was as meticulously kept as she, although, on this particular day, she was thinking of taking up a former bad habit and filling the car's ash tray with coral-printed filters on the butts of fags she had smoked. She was on edge, shaky, the twists of her coif slightly wispy, like the frayed nerves she so tightly held inside the emotions she rarely let loose. She had let loose this morning, though, before doing her usual ablutions and her make-up to step into the Cadillac and drive not to the high school, where she would be expected after the weekend, but north, to some indeterminate place—she knew not where.

When she saw the figure in the distance, on the side of the highway, she knew immediately what she would do. And, even though Clista was nothing like the sort to pick up a hitchhiker, she would certainly make an exception on this day, as she put her life, her profession, her town behind her, making a sure-to-be futile attempt to run away. This was a day of making all kinds of breaks, the shattering of facades, the clattering of realities, a day to step out of character and try to locate her self, if there ever was such a thing. It made a crazy kind of ironic sense to pick up a hitcher, who, as she drew closer, looked more and more like a teenage girl, finally becoming one, sturdy but slight of frame, like a gymnast. Certainly not threatening, like the haggard and tattooed serial killer stereotype that had forever lived in her wagons-circled mind. She pulled to the shoulder of the road and watched in the rearview mirror as the girl gathered up her things and bounded toward the waiting vehicle, then, catching her own eyes in the reflecting oval of silvered glass, saw a shadow of the emotion and primal fear that had captured Clista in the pre-dawn hours this morning, when she shot and killed her husband of forty-something years.

It was only an oddity to her now that she had done such a thing; it seemed distant and sketchily surreal. Strange how rapidly those tautly-bound emotions came undone, ramping into the kind of sight-blotted rage that would allow a person to do murder, settling afterwards into a numbness of spirit and mind that allowed her to believe in the possibility of, simply, running away—to almost believe it never happened in the first place. The numbness vibrated in an ear-humming buzz, as if her entire skull were swaddled in layer upon layer of cotton sheeting or felt, but there were fuzzy sounds of car doors and heavy canvas bags thudding into the leather seats. Then a voice, a face, something like words.

"What?" Clista managed.

"It's just that you've saved my life, that's all. If I had to be in this nothing place just one more day, just one more day, I would go nut case. See, my family is an insane asylum. My dope fiend mother especially. And so I just now packed up my shit, marched my butt down that dirt lane, and sat myself on the side of the highway. And here you come right off the bat. Shit, what's your name?"

It was a jarring question, and inside of Clista's hesitation, her guest continued.

"I'm Savannah. But I don't think I'll keep that name. Doesn't sound bluesy enough. Sa-van-nah. It's a city in Georgia. Which is known for peaches. But what about Georgia? For a name, I mean."

Clista was still thinking about her own name.

"Do you have any chips or something?" The girl had not taken a breath. "I'm always hungry. I'm definitely set on a different speed than most other people. Are you going to put it in drive?"

Again the out-of-left-field questions caught Clista off guard. "I—yes," she said, pulling back onto the pavement. Ever prepared for emergencies, she gestured at the glove box, where Savannah found a pack of cheese crackers.

The girl tore into the package with her teeth, orange crumbs scattering, then, "I love states for names—Bama, Carolina. Cities, not so much. Missouri is nice. What's yours?"

"My—"

"Name."

"It's Clista," she said, thinking, and I murdered my husband this morning, because he did the unimaginable and betrayed our decades of sameness and safety and "understoods," and "inasmuches" and such immaculate respectability as most

156

couples never achieve. He took all that was invested in our public presentation as a couple and crumbled every iota of trust into talcum powder and the fairy dust that magically transformed me into a cold, cold killer.

"—so of course you know that," Savannah was saying.

"Know what?"

"What I was saying. Are you alright? I was saying how your name sounds something like a female part, but I guess you caught a lot of teasing at a certain age, so of course you know that. Junior high is hell for everybody." She sucked in a breath. "I'm sorry if I offended you. Sometimes I go over the top. My mind goes faster than I can talk and I try to keep up and so words get blurted out before I know it. You know?"

Clista was not accustomed to such talk, talk of female parts with sexual references, cursing, and just plain chattiness of a distasteful bent, as she had no good best girlfriend, having kept the world at a polite, respectable distance. This girl, however, felt unthreatening in spite of her verbiage. "How old are you?" the driver attempted to divert.

"Twenty-six," was the reply. "I know, I know. I look sixteen. I get it all the time. It's because I'm so small-boned. And flat chested. I've thought about store-bought tits, implants, but I just don't believe in doing that shit to your body." She sighed with a flourish. "It's a blessing and a curse, being my size. I mean, when I tell people I'm a blues singer, they laugh. 'Ain't no big, bluesy voice gonna come out of that little thing.' Plus I'm white, obviously. 'Little bitty white chicks can't sing the blues.' Folks just don't take me seriously. When you've lived through the low down dirty shit I've lived through, you can damn sure feel the hurt. Like, what do you do when it takes your crack head mother two years to get rid of a man who's pushing his hands in your panties and you're nine years old? Two years!"

"Oh, my!" Clista drew away from her, an instinct, and was immediately embarrassed.

"Well, it wasn't my fault, you know."

"Of course not. Absolutely not. I'm so sorry. I'm just not accustomed—"

"My point is, that's just one of the crappy things I've experienced. And it wasn't even the worst. But I keep it upbeat, you know? Keep it in the sunlight. Positive thoughts. Let it out in the lyrics. So do you believe I can sing?"

"I would imagine so," Clista said, thinking instead that betrayal felt like the big, silver blade of a very sharp knife slicing cleanly through the jugular. He betrayed me and I was unleashed in an unthinkable way, into utter insanity. I was not responsible, nor do I regret. The lioness kills to protect her vulnerable offspring, after all. Is there an analogy to be had? Does it even matter?

"—and my boyfriend—he's a tattoo artist—he did all of mine, see?" She turned her leg to reveal the serpent-like lizard inked around her calf, winding toward its own tail; turned a shoulder bearing a crucifix, Jesus and his blood upon an elaborately detailed cross, the eyes of the holy martyr cast up in surrender to the Father. "His name—my boyfriend's—is Dakota. A state, right? It fits with my world view. He is amazingly talented. I mean, isn't this gorgeous?" She pulled down the front of her t-shirt to reveal, just above her heart, a small but beautifully intricate insect of some kind—something like one might find in a fly fisherman's tackle box. "I have others, but they are in hard to find places, if you know what I mean."

Clista's husband was a fly fisherman with a vast, three-tiered tackle box loaded with treasured lures, some even from his navy days, the days of their courtship. He took regular and frequent fishing trips to Colorado at solitary resorts, to the Rocky Mountain streams where he danced his line in the rhythmic ballet of a cast. She did not accompany him as she had no interest in his hobbies other than as fodder for those sometimes necessary social conversations:

"Paul loves his lures as much as he loves me," she might joke, "but at least he finds me more alluring." Not that she alluded to any sort of physical sensuality between the two of them. Clista had always found that particular expression of human instinct to be distasteful at best, more of the time disgusting. There were un-artful fumblings early in their union, a marriage that followed a courteous courtship, but they soon settled into a life of platonic rhythms, ebbing away into separate workdays, flowing back into their isolated split-level home in the evenings. And no later than ten p.m. they would be tucked into twin beds connected by a night stand bearing an antique Princess telephone, pink, with a nine millimeter loaded and at the ready in its French Provincial drawer.

"—so why don't you just take a look," Savannah had opened a cell phone and was scrolling through some photographs. "Here you go," and she turned the screen to Clista.

"Oh!" It came almost as a shriek paired with another recoiling of her whole body. The wheels left the blacktop for a few seconds.

"Holy Christ—what was that?" Savannah looked at her as if she had two heads and then studied the screen of her phone, a close-up of her pubic area and the peace lily engraved above the curls. Her face fell. "Oh. I thought you wanted to see my other tattoos. Sorry."

"No, it's alright. I—I'm just not accustomed to such images."

"No shit. Well, I didn't mean to scare you. I mean, it's just skin, basically. I've never seen what the big deal is. Skin is skin. It holds in our organs. Sex is something else, but it really amounts to just rubbing. But you're the driver so I sure as hell won't fuck with you. But you have to know up front that I was born without a filter."

"Filter?"

"You know, I tend to blurt out whatever's in my head. I'm ADHD, so it kind of goes with the territory. I'll try to watch my mouth, though. I mean, you could easily just dump me on the side of the road again. And there I'd be with my thumb out. Again."

"I won't do that." Then, for no real reason she could fathom, she added, "I'm going all the way to Memphis."

"For real? Holy shit, that's awesome. How lucky is it you picked me up? And don't worry—no more tattoo pictures," and she laughed a trilling, lively laugh.

Paul had a tattoo, from the time he served in the navy during the Vietnam Conflict. It was of two intertwining snakes encircling a cross, the word "Bound" crowning the top of the cross like a bent halo. He said it represented his love of country, how bound up in it he was. And he believed in what he was doing in fighting the Red Menace off the shores of Southeast Asia, even if he never had to dodge any bullets.

"Your husband?"

"What?" Clista had not realized she had spoken.

"The serpents. So symbolic. I mean, my Uncle Jessie

actually fought over there—lost a leg and an eye. He has a cool glass eye he always entertained us with—my cousins and me—when we were kids. He'd take it out and toss it up in the air and catch it in his mouth like popcorn."

Clista shuddered.

"I know, pretty gross. But not if you're a little kid and not really at all if you think. I mean, look what he's been through. He deserves to do whatever the hell he wants, huh? He doesn't have a fake leg anymore. He used to. And he could make it do fart noises, another thing little kids love."

"Goodness!" Paul was not allowed—had not been allowed—to fart in her presence. Clista insisted that he step into the bathroom or outside if that urge was upon him. On those occasions when it happened serendipitously, he apologized with abject humiliation to her stony disdain.

Black earth was turned in the fields bordering Highway 61. It was planting time and within months the black dirt would turn to snow, and cotton puffs would litter the roadside after picking was done. Picking. To pick off. She had killed him, shot him in the head right there in his study, where she had found him before dawn, crept up to the door, borne witness to the sounds of lecherous, staccato-rhythmed motions and gritty, profane talk. He was preoccupied enough not to notice the slight click as she eased the door open, just a crack, just enough that she could see the man facing him on the computer screen, knew immediately who he was—the man in the photographs holding stringers heavy-laden with fish—the best friend from the navy, Spencer Kraus, also married. She fetched the gun and returned to wait it out. He did not notice, even when the screen had gone dark and he had lain his head down on his arms, exhausted, as she padded across the carpet's soft pile in one dreamlike motion, squeezed two bullets into his skull, turned and left just that quickly, with the stealth of a jungle cat.

"So tell me more." Savannah's words, again jarring.

"What do you mean?"

"You just said you were a cat."

"What?"

"Yeah, a jungle cat. And I'm thinking, what the hell?"

"I'm sorry," Clista stammered. "I'm just upset." She had to watch her words, slipping out unintended and quick, like minnows darting across currents.

"Well, then tell it, sister. What did the son of a bitch do?" She pulled out a pack of American Spirit cigarettes. "Okay if I smoke?"

"Yes." Her surrender felt like the beginning of some kind of relief. "But only if you light one for me."

✳

The sound of clattering dishes and running water came from a kitchen in the back of the diner. Savannah was putting heart and soul into devouring her sandwich, dousing it mid-chew and frequently with Dr. Pepper. "Thank you so much for buying," she gulped. "My money situation is pretty busy, but that'll change when I hook up with Dakota."

Clista had attempted to force down a salad, but nausea made that impossible so she nibbled a couple of Saltines. She had bought her very own pack of cigarettes, Virginia Slim menthols, the brand of her younger years. You've come a long way, Baby, the old advertising jingle rattled around in her head. She exhaled a mushroom cloud of smoke. "I can't think, can't know what to do."

"Sure you can." Savannah leaned across the table, speaking in a hushed but animated tone. "You can absolutely know what to do. You just have to connect all the dots. That's what My Uncle Jessie used to say, anyway. But he was pretty PTSD. You're probably kind of PTSD about now, too."

"The dots are scattered, all across the floor," and she thought of throwing jacks as a child, the scattering stars, the ball bouncing. "That's the way the ball bounces," she murmured, smiling.

"Okay, okay, you're not going all mental on me, right?"

"No. I've already been mental. Can I go sane on you?"

"That would be good, but dude, your life is going to go end over end either way. I mean, you've got to either get a new identity and disappear—and that's really hard—or go back and come clean—and that's really hard, too. Man!" and her eyes widened at the enormity of it all.

"Are my eyes still red and puffy?"

"Yeah, but that's good. I think it keeps the waitress from coming over too often."

Clista took out her compact and applied a fresh coat of coral to her lips. I am a coral snake. She blotted with a napkin pulled from the stainless steel holder.

They were in a desolate part of the state where the crook of the Mississippi separated Arkansas, Tennessee and Mississippi, at Buck's Diner, where time had stopped decades earlier, an eatery with worn red plastic seats, dull chrome, and a hanging musk of aged bacon grease. It was just past the lunch hour, so the two women had the place to themselves while a sour-faced teenager bussed a few tables. A grizzled looking cook sat at a booth near the kitchen door, smoking, chatting in a low, gravelly voice with the one waitress, who sauntered over to the travelers once in a while, called them "honey" and "sugar" and "baby" as she offered more tea.

"Man, you're in some serious shit. I've known all kinds of people slogging through all kinds of shit. Hell, my own mother only had me because she couldn't afford another abortion. She was a drug addict. Cocaine. Sometimes she did men to get money for it. Now she's killing herself with meth. I was trying to help her get straight, but that stuff is insane. In-fucking-sane. You really saved my life by picking me up."

A hopeful little ripple went through Clista. "Do you think maybe that cancels out the other?"

"Maybe so," Savannah grinned. "Maybe the karma is right now. Maybe that's a reason to keep running. Or to go back."

"I can't believe I actually told you everything. It's not like me at all."

"But it is me. Seriously. It's something about me," Savannah said. "People tell me stuff all the time. Strangers. I mean, I'll be in the check out line and somebody will just unload their whole entire bizarre life story. It happens all the freaking time."

But I don't confide in anyone, Clista thought, still marveling at how Savannah had coaxed the darkness out of her.

"What did the son of a bitch do?" she had asked.

"How do you know it's about a man?"

"Always is. Your husband?"

"Yes."

"So come on with it."

"No."

"Come on. Tell it."

"I can't."

"Just say the words."

And Clista's fingers had tightened on the steering wheel of the smoke-filled champagne-colored Cadillac. "My husband betrayed me."

"You know it."

"He lied and cheated and did it from the start."

"Uh-huh."

"And it's worse than that."

"How?"

"My husband betrayed me."

"Tell."

"With a man."

"Holy Christ."

"A double life."

"You're right. That is worse. Way fucking worse."

"I was faithful to that man forever and he was faithful to his man forever and I caught him in a despicable act and I killed him."

"Killed?"

"Shot."

"The fuck you say!" And Savannah had turned her body fully facing her in the car. "You are so not the type!"

"Apparently I am." And she had pulled onto the shoulder of the road, rested her head on the steering wheel and howled like a wounded animal as Savannah, effervescence disarmed by the rawness of it all, tried impotently to console her.

The waitress sauntered over. "Here, Sweetie, let me get this out of your way," and began collecting plates and utensils, blood red fingernails clicking against heavy white glass.

Savannah picked up the last of her BLT and pushed the plate. "Are you still taking me to Memphis?" she asked as the waitress sauntered away.

"Of course."

"You're not, like, dangerous or anything, right?" It was almost a whisper.

"I have no weapons or designs upon your possessions."

"I know that. It just felt like a question I had to ask, you know? I mean, how dumb would I feel if something really happened—and I know it isn't—but something happened and I never even asked the question in the first place. Man, would I feel dumb."

"Certainly."

"Plus, I just got to get to Memphis."

What will you do when you get to there? Where will you live?"

"With Dakota, of course. He'll come pick me up wherever you and I land. He has a place off Beale Street, right in the thick of things. Man, I can't wait to go out to some of those clubs. Not the touristy ones on the main drag. The real ones. The ones you have to just happen into. But the first thing I'm going to do—and I know this is stupid and touristy and all—but I'm going to get me some barbecue."

"Can I join you?"

"Sure. Are you like, buying?"

"Of course. It'll be my last supper."

"Holy shit. You're not going all suicidal or anything, are you? Because that's even more messed up than what's gone down. Seriously."

"You're right. Besides, I don't know. Could I actually go home to that—mess, and put the gun to my own head? I just don't see it."

"Well, you know they say it's a permanent solution to a temporary problem, right?"

"It would certainly be a problem for both my permanent and my temple," Clista said, but her puny, half-hearted attempt at punning fell on deaf ears.

✳

Memphis was a presence she could feel well before hitting the outskirts. It was in the whispery thrum of potential stories in song—a spiritual imprint that webbed out and out to the rising hills and farms, cascading down the Mississippi River to rich Delta dirt.

Savannah must have felt it, too. She threw her head back and let fly several bars of melodic anguish, big and rich, at odds with the tiny vessel making the music. "You might think you're living large, baby, but you'll be dying when you get home. You might think you're hitting the mark, baby, but you'll just be trying when you get home." She turned to Clista. "What do you think? It's something I've been working on."

"You're very talented. I don't know a lot about the blues, but you have a unique sound."

"Unique good or unique I-can't-think-of anything-good-to-say-so-I'll-say-unique?"

"Definitely good. Raspy good."

Savannah beamed. "Thank you. And you're wrong about the other."

"What other?"

"The blues. You know a hell of a lot about the blues."

"I do? Well, yes, now."

"No, always. Can you talk about your life? Your self? I mean, okay, you spent a very long marriage being some guy's beard, but that doesn't happen in a vacuum, you know?"

"A beard?"

"You know the wife of a gay man who lives in a really deep closet."

"There's actually slang for it?"

"Sure. You don't know a lot about sex, do you?"

"I know it's messy."

"Okay, see, this is what I mean. You don't like sex. That's how you and your husband connected, on a really basic level. So if you think about it, it was not a bad arrangement. You each got what you needed. You just couldn't handle knowing it, right?"

"I'm not sure. What I've done is so much worse than knowing anything."

"Who really knows anything?"

"What do you mean?"

"Well, my boyfriend Dakota, right? He believes that there is nothing but thought and that we've thought all this up. Like, you thought me up on the side of the road and poof, there I was. You thought up a husband who used you as his beard so you killed him."

"This is all a lot of pseudo-philosophical malarkey."

"Oh my god, you said 'malarkey.' You are so not the type to kill a person. But anyway, here's the thing."

"I suppose I could just think him back alive, correct?"

"Well?"

"You must be crazy."

"Yeah, I am, but so is everybody—including you."

Clista's muscle memory sprang into a mode of defense that immediately fizzled. Crazy? With such a buffed and polished image? With a picture perfect life? With the dead husband laid out across his computer desk? "Maybe I can think him back alive?"

"Damn right. It's got to be worth a freaking try."

They ate just outside the city limits at Uncle Stumpy's Bodacious Barbecue Bin, thick brown sauce crawling across their fingers, down their chins, sticky napkins piled on the tabletop. Clista found herself laughing at the mess of it all. "This is real barbecue. I've never had the real thing," and she sucked on her fingers just like Savannah did. And when Savannah flipped open her cell phone to call boyfriend Dakota to come and pick her up, Clista studied the way the young woman cocked her head, trilled her voice up and down, like a delightful little bird, as she spoke. Twenty-six, yet so much like a young girl—enthusiastic, forward looking, hopeful, on the verge of a dream.

They embraced in the parking lot. "I never knew," Clista said. "How could I not know?"

"But didn't you, really? Come on, didn't you? Way down deep? In your guts?

Clista opened her purse and withdrew the compact and tube of coral lipstick. "I guess that's a thing to consider." She reapplied her signature color, pulled out a Kleenex and blotted a kiss onto it. She folded the Kleenex and handed it to Savannah. "If you're ever really low, give yourself a kiss from me."

"Oh, I've already been plenty low. I'm aiming for up now. But, just in case, thanks."

"You'll be okay here?" Clista glanced around the parking lot. It was not the best neighborhood, judging by the buildings in various stages of disrepair, and day had fallen into dusk.

"Oh, hell yeah. Dakota won't be too long."

"But it's getting dark and you're unfamiliar with the area." There was a pharmacy across the street that was well-lit. "You should go to the bench by that drug store."

Savannah giggled. "Are you kidding? Nothing's going to happen to me. You should know this about me by now. No point in letting worry rule your world, huh?"

"I guess."

"So have you decided what you're going to do?"

"Yes, I have."

"And it feels right?"

"Yes."

"Good."

The champagne colored Cadillac was warm from the sunlight trapped inside just a short time ago—invisible but there, the traces of a star. Clista rolled down the windows and waved as she waited to pull out of the parking lot. She looked back for a few seconds longer to see Savannah arrange her possessions and plop down on her duffel bag next to the front of the rib joint, a snapshot of a reality Clista had enjoyed for a day. She wasn't sure if the woman—no, the girl—was a chance that fell out of the sky or a providential event sent by some spiritual presence in an effort to set things right. Maybe the girl really would fade from existence once Clista turned away, so she hesitated for a moment, not wanting that vibrancy to dissipate, like the rays of the sun were.

"Just go!" Savannah shouted, waving her off, laughing.

Clista giggled, a genuine sound, pressed the gas, and pulled away. She started to roll up the windows, but caught herself, even told herself "No," right out loud. Then, at a glimpse of her eyes in the rear-view mirror, she even whispered, "You crazy fucker."

And she left the windows down into the evening, rolling south through the farm country, past the scrubby towns and lives of folks left behind. The push of air blew a rhythm of comfort into her soul, disengaging strands of platinum blonde that whipped about her face, growing into a small hurricane of color-treated hair spiraling around the eye of coral lips. She would drive well into the night, until she made it all the way home, consuming every millisecond with the fierce energy of thinking, thinking hard, thinking him back alive.

The Good Sister

She was the eldest of nine and therefore the substitute mother to many, those in the middle in particular, beginning when she was barely seven. And of course the middle shifted pretty much yearly, or whenever her mother's belly grew round and ripe. They lived in a four bedroom two story with a dog and a cat, a washing machine that seemed to never stop washing, one bathroom for all the children, and another for parents only. There had to be blood or imminent vomiting or diarrhea for that rule to be relaxed. Otherwise, urges were to be controlled and the mandate was clear that the children's bathroom was to be used efficiently. That is, with no shut door and multiple users at different tasks, as necessary.

She was happy to help out because the nuns at St. Mary's Catholic Girls' School said that faith without good works was a dead and useless faith. The parable of the Good Samaritan was one of her favorites; it made perfect sense to a child with a pure heart. And she was happy to do unto others, following The Golden Rule that hung in every classroom.

St. Mary's was her favorite place, the one place she could really and truly be a child—or rather, attempt to be one. But even as she grabbed onto the steel clutch at the end of a chain, and ran to gather enough speed to fly around the maypole, even as she roamed the monkey bars, jumping from square to square, her squeals of laughter and her giggles bore tonal differences—varying octaves, underlying melodies, odd rest notes, something very unlike the delightful sounds of other children. If one of the boys skinned a knee or fell from a tree limb on the playground only to come up with a gashed forehead, she was the one who comforted him and took him to the nuns, walked with them to the school nurse, her arm curled around his shoulder. If one of the girls became ill in class, she was the one who helped her to the restroom and held back her hair, saying soothing words while the girl threw up into the tiny toilet. Her experiences had evolved into a demeanor, a carriage, that said she was already wired to be a mother, after hours upon hours of diaper changing, rash nursing, nose wiping, book reading, stroller rolling, lullaby singing, bottle warming, rattle shaking and all things infant, toddler, little one.

And she loved her siblings, every one of them, though like any honest mother she had to admit she played favorites. She grew automatically partial to the newest born, each and every time, could not resist the petal-soft skin, Gerber-baby mouths, scents of Johnson's Powder and Baby Oil, and the innocent, sweet eyes that gazed deep into hers. Of course, she could offer no real competition to the one who gave birth and was always relegated to second-degree mom status, herding and tending as much of the brood as her young years allowed. Aside from the newborns, her favorite was the Fifth Born, the third amongst the boys, who were of a different class than the girls, but not in the early years, when they had to mind her and the other surrogates. She could only guess, as she grew up, as to why her strongest affection leaned toward the Fifth Born of nine, the third of five boys. Maybe it was the endearing way he sucked his thumb, self-comforting in the din of child sounds. Maybe it was because he seemed the most lost and unnoticed within the herd, although by the time he was four he had figured out how to demand notice by making mischief. He pranked, provoked, finagled and weaseled his way into more, she figured, than a few harsh punishments, more than the other boys combined. Her mother's wrath fell upon the Fifth Born, with his practical jokester ways, wrapped up in one word: deceit.

Over the years, this label officially stamped the Fifth Born a liar. So the Good Sister made extra efforts to tend to him, extra time with books, with toys on the floor, playing games. She taught him to draw using the "Peanuts" comic strips from the funny papers every Sunday afternoon, Snoopy and Charlie Brown and Linus with his blue blanket taking shape on lined spiral notebook paper. Bonus hugs were bestowed upon him, attempts at inoculating him with a vaccine to prevent, she must have felt on a primal gut level, self-loathing, a word she could not have known.

It was not too difficult to make extra hours for the Fifth Born. By the time she was eleven and he six, there were third- and fourth-degree moms to do her bidding. Three girls, woven in amongst the first four boys, upon whom the family's real hopes were pegged. Her parents expected that all of their sons would be altar boys and that at least one, or more, please God, would follow destiny when called to the priesthood. She knew that there were no expectations that she would be an altar girl, though; there were no such things. The highest expectation of her and her sisters was that they be good surrogate mothers, get postsecondary educations, marry well, marry within The Church of course, and have their own broods of babies bred of good stock and righteous faith.

When her mother was not rigidly barking orders and keeping schedules and administering punishments, she was distant and aloof, although her husband brought laughter and music and dance into the family realm, entertaining the brood by firing up the Zenith Hi-Fi Stereo, putting on record after record, and performing ballroom dances like the waltz and the cha-cha and the tango with his bride. "She could have been a Rockette!" he would exclaim, a puff of pride in his cry. His wife rolled her eyes and blushed, but followed that with a faraway gaze that watched well past the modestly furnished living room where the threadbare wool rug had been rolled back for the frivolity. "Yes," the look appeared to say, "I could have." And it seemed to the Good Sister that her mother's distance grew after each of these infrequent courtings by her father, as he tried to draw a bit of joy from the woman he clearly loved but who, though she must have loved him back, could not let loose with those tender emotions as easily as he.

Even though *Time* had recently declared that God was dead, the Good Sister clung to the teachings of the nuns, prayed the Rosary every day, and attended weekly Mass with her entire family, knowing that God was, indeed, real, and that she would be with Jesus in Heaven one day. She would also be there with the one baby sister who died, who could not stay in her mother's belly long enough to grow. Angela.

The Good Sister imagined Angela with long golden hair and large green eyes, with soft little palms and ticklish toes. She had cast her unborn sister in the role of princess among the angels, decreed to be eternally four years old, because that seemed a magical age.

All the girls in the family attended St. Mary's Catholic Girls' School while the boys attended the prestigious St. Ignatius Catholic Boys' School, all on scholarship, sporting button-down shirts, khaki pants, navy coats and ties. It was an honor, their mother said, and would get them into good colleges one day. "You mind the Brothers and keep out of trouble. Do not bring shame on this family."

The Fifth Born presumably tried but found himself in front of the Headmaster often, for silly pranks or scorning authority or failing to do homework, so he was often banned from family nights of TV, often not allowed to play outdoors with neighborhood children in the hours after school.

Approaching the age of twelve, the Good Sister attended Catechism classes to prepare for her Confirmation. There she learned more about the Saints and the Miracles and the mysterious logic of the Holy Trinity. For the grand rite of passage, her mother sewed a beautiful white cotton eyelet empire dress with bell sleeves over silk, bought her a luxurious French lace veil that they could barely afford, her mother reminded her, but it was for the church. The Good Sister carried a white bible beneath her rosary beads and felt a sense of pomp and grandness when she filed into the cathedral with the other girls. And the scapula she would wear, always, bore the countenance and name of Saint Margaret, patron saint of pregnant women, for the fathers and the nuns thought it genuine and kind that she would honor Angela in such a way.

The white bible and French lace would become the standard confirmation gifts for each succeeding daughter, since it would not be fair to favor one child over another. The boys got standard issue black bibles, which made the Good Sister feel special, as if there were something girls had over the opposite sex. In this way she felt she was more of an intimate with the Holy Mother Mary, something a boy could never truly be.

The next three boys, including the Fifth Born, were also confirmed and did, indeed, become altar boys by the time she was seventeen. She was proud of them as they rang and dampened the bells during the Latin service, or held the gold tray of wafers beneath the congregants' chins, mouths of the faithful gaping open like hungry baby birds. "May the body of Christ be with you," the priest would murmur, initiating the response ritual. She loved the way the Fifth Born, especially, looked so somber and holy in his long black cassock with the surplus on top, pouring water and wine into the elaborate gold chalice held by the Monsignor. She got goose bumps when the boys chanted in Latin, their innocent sing-song voices a stark contrast to the deep voices of the men who called to them, and she was happy that her family's congregation was bound and determined to defy Vatican II and conduct the Mass just as it had for centuries. And they would also refuse to eat meat on any Friday, thank you very much.

The Good Sister knew it was a joke among her brothers and the other altar boys that when it came time to fill the chalice the Monsignor would have one of them pour wine and a seeming forever would pass before the cleric would give the ever so subtle signal to stop, by raising the vessel just a hair. Then the bearer of the water decanter would begin, only to get the signal to stop after a mere splash. They all knew that the priests had to drain the chalice of all that was left after communion, that none of it could be reused and that the two church leaders were likely tipsy enough after that.

The two priests at St. Ignatius Cathedral were a younger one, fresh from the seminary, who was serious but not stand-offish, and The Old Father, the Monsignor, who laughed large and tickled the girls and mussed the boys' hair, and made funny faces at the toddlers to the delight of their mothers. As they approached adolescence, though, he was more hands-off as he guided them toward confirmation and the true gravity of being a faithful congregant. It was not to be taken lightly, he said, and he conferred with the boys privately, while the nuns took individual girls under their counsel.

Sometimes the Good Sister thought how wonderful it would be to become a nun, married to the Lord, wearing the billowing habit, the beautiful gold cross at her hip. Some of the sisters at St. Mary's were very stern, though most seemed kind enough, and a few were even beautiful, like the one in that Haley Mills movie, *The Trouble With Angels*. They were all, however, mysterious, with their private rituals, spiritual wedding bands, and secretive airs. But as much as the Good Sister wished to marry the Mystery, be as pure as they, she knew in her heart that she wanted to be a mother, always, and if she were ever to go into a convent as a novice she would surely be wooed away by some handsome man, as Julie Andrews was in *The Sound of Music*.

Sundays were a rambunctious time, before and after Mass, the rounding up of bibles and rosaries, making sure all the children's feet were shrouded in matching socks and dress shoes, petticoats in stiff silhouettes, neckties and hair bows and finery as if in preparation for a pilgrimage to Rome. And once the service was over, a flurry of undoing, the three boys, including the Fifth Born, wresting free of their full skirts in the anteroom of the Old Father's sanctuary. It was on such a typical Sunday that the family station wagon was found light of one sibling, the Fifth Born--not an unusual thing for this particular brother, free of spirit, with a tendency to roam the hallways and balconies of the huge building, to go missing. He was off with friends, wrestling on the back lawn, or exploring what might be hidden passages full of ancient treasures, or plundering the wine and wafers.

The Good Sister immediately attended to the task of gathering up one of her lost biddies. She went directly to the Old Father's sanctuary, fully expecting to find it empty of anyone, but as she entered she felt an oddness in the air, and her body willed her to slow down, to be quiet, the instinct of a lioness welling up, unconsciously uneasy. She approached the heavy oak door of the sacristy, where the accouterments and unsanctified communion wafers were kept. Ornately carved with cherubs and rosebuds, the door was chained on the other side, but carelessly, enough that it was caught open, the doorknob latch disengaged. It was open enough for her to hear, and then to see, through the sliver of access. And then to scream to the emptiness of the building, to push against the door, to hear the fumblings and murmurs and rushing of the Old Father, the clattering of the chain that echoed and held, it seemed, forever.

When the chain latch was finally released, the stark white collar hung in the air above her head like a guillotine's blade, as if it could slice all of her spirit and comforts to shreds, but she felt strangely apathetic about that, and her claws must have been bared in her expression. Because the Old Father said nothing when she snatched the Fifth Born by the arm and spirited him away to the family coach, holding in, holding in, until she could stand before her parents, alone, and sob out what she had witnessed. Was she sure? Yes. How could she know? Because she was almost eighteen, ready to leave for nursing school and didn't they know teenage girls talked? Didn't they know teenage boys lusted and that she had been privy to some limited experience with that? Didn't they know how different the world was now, after The Pill and free love? Which turned their rage upon her. What did she know about The Pill? She knew some girls who took it but she would never, ever. What had she been up to? Nothing serious, just silly dates. Anyway, she was committed to chastity and what about the Fifth Born?

The Fifth Born was then brought in to that inner sanctum that was his parents' bedroom, where the whole lot of them had supposedly been conceived in mysterious intimacy that yielded miracles of life. Her brother was closely questioned, was vague in his responses, confused, ashamed, tearful, having neither the vocabulary, at thirteen years of age, nor the inclination to delve into what all the fuss was. And the Good Sister looked on, feeling she should have done something sooner, wondering why she had not prevented it, certain she was at fault, but that she alone could not be to blame, could she? She closed her eyes to attempt an escape from racing thoughts, but that white collar flashed into the darkness, so stark and unyielding, that she opened them for relief, only to find her brother's vacant gaze. She wanted to hold him, beg his forgiveness, do some kind of penance, and believe that she could hope to regain a sense of peace.

The first three, now four, brothers were abruptly withdrawn from St. Ignatius Catholic Boys' School and enrolled in public school, and the siblings found themselves deposited in a new church, St. Mary's. No explanations were ever offered, and the Good Sister never broke that implied vow of silence. She did not even have to be given that directive.

She left home for nursing school, studying human anatomy, physiology, and infection control, attending the small Catholic church in the little college town. She thought to speak to the priest about what had happened, make confession about her lack of diligence and the shattering repercussions of that failure. There were many evenings when she would stand before her dresser mirror, practicing what she would say. "Forgive me Father, for I have sinned." And she would piece together any number of awkward words, cobble together enough phrasings that would get out the gist of it, and even though she ended up in tears, she would promise herself that next Sunday would be the day. Instead, she could never scrape up the nerve to face her sins and always, of any Sunday, felt queasy and clammy and inadequate upon entering the foyer of the church.

When she visited home during breaks and for holidays, she was greeted with elaborately drawn posters made by the Fifth Born, featuring Charlie Brown, Snoopy and the gang, meticulously colored, with "WELCOME HOME!" in all caps and dedication. She knew he must have spent hours on the detail, was proud that he was such a fine artist, hoped that he would find solace someday, in art. She always made a big fuss over his efforts and made a point of taking the posters back to school, to hang them in her dorm room.

"I wish he would put as much effort into his school work," his mother said.

But the whimsical images of the "Peanuts" gang gradually began to close in on her—Linus with that thumb to his mouth, Pigpen shrouded in a billowing cloud of dirt, Lucy with her vicious football, forever betraying good ol' Charlie Brown's trust, and Snoopy doing his famous "happy dance" amidst it all. With her dorm room covered over in the colorful Lost Children, for the adults were never anywhere to be seen in the "Peanuts" strips, she slipped into an emptiness that must, she thought, feel like the death of a child. She developed migraine headaches that threw her into a fetal position every time, and she feared her skull would break wide open and ooze its contents onto the bed. She withdrew from school and informed her parents that she wanted to come home.

Her mother and father drove to the little college and confronted her. This was unacceptable. They were simply not having it, they told her, asking her what kind of trouble she had fallen into. Was she failing? No, although her heart told her she was. Was she giving in to poor peer influences? No, she told them, she did not socialize much. Then why? Oh no, Holy Mother of Jesus, was she pregnant? And that drove the Good Sister into a sudden gale of laughter, so much laughter that she had trouble stopping, even as her parents demanded it.

How could she laugh in the face of such a situation?

She was sorry, she told them.

They were terribly disappointed in her, they said. What

about the family expectation of a postsecondary education? Sorry. How would they explain it to their friends? Sorry. How would they bear the shame? Sorry. They did not want apologies, they wanted explanations, and she had better offer one right this minute, young lady. To which the Good Sister lay down on the bed in her dorm room, on her back, hands crossed at her breast, like a corpse, eyes closed, and whispered repeatedly that she could not be in that room another minute, confounding them with such uncharacteristically odd and rebellious behavior. They loaded her into the station wagon and drove her home.

As the Good Sister unpacked her suitcases in her new old bedroom, the Fifth Born flipped through the old posters he had made. She complimented him, again, on his talent, but turned to him with tears and a look of defeat on her face. "I know this is you," she said, pointing to Linus. "And this," pointing to Pig Pen, and on through the other symbols that had seeped into her consciousness over the months. "But this," and she pulled a happy-dancing Snoopy out of the stack. "I have to know. Is this who you wish you were?"

He could only look down at his hands and shrug. "I'm fine," he said.

It wasn't long before her mother was happy to have the Good Sister's help once again, with the stair steps that now ranged from her eldest, at nineteen, all the way down to a surprise, pre-menopausal infant of eighteen months. That Ninth Child stirred real physical murmurings, hormonal sea-changes, even uterine contractions, and when she found the menstrual excretions, she wondered if she were really fit to be a mother. She wondered even more as she watched the Fifth Child, with his glib attitude, his academic laziness, his eyes red and puffy from the pot he smoked as often as he and his friends could get it, which was pretty much continuously. Their parents, though, were oblivious to anything but the superficial, such as poor grades. So the Good Sister tried to talk to him, not about the past, but the present and his future. She loved him, she said, and was worried. To which he would each time and always ever after respond by giving her a bear hug, a cheek kiss, and saying "Don't worry about me. I'm just fine."

But the Good Sister did not believe him, and that "I'm just fine," became a humming buzz in her head, which grew into a migraine until she had to take the pills that had been prescribed by the campus physician back at the little college. She would go to bed, blotting out the light with a sleep mask, the cacophonous family sounds with the white noise of an oscillating fan, hoping for sleep to keep her shame at bay. She would emerge to only repeat the cycle—the holding of the Ninth Born, the subsequent maternal yearnings, and then the doubt and self-hatred and feelings of loss, until she decided to lock herself in the bathroom, a bathroom whose door was never closed, for in a household of nine children modesty could have no purchase. And she lit a candle and swallowed all that remained in the bottle of prescription migraine pills along with some sweet red wine in her own private communion.

At the hospital, her parents told her how the door had to be battered in, how the ambulance had to deliver her to the ER to get her stomach pumped, and how could she? Didn't she know it was a mortal sin? Whatever could have driven her to do this to the family? But the Fifth Born held her hand and squeezed it and told her everything would be okay, and she almost found herself believing him. "I love you," she said, and he gifted her with a smile.

A church deacon was sent to counsel her, to reassure her that she was not a fallen soul, that God truly did have the grace to forgive, that she could repent and reclaim her salvation. He was stoic but kind, several years older, but very young for a deacon so he must be a good Catholic. He did not press her for details when she told him the church had failed her and she had failed her brother and hinted at the details. They talked in a strange kind of code, as if not daring to lay too much bare, needing to keep it in some subterraneous place, where secrets were at bay but living, some place like hell, she thought. The Deacon convinced her that with effort and prayer she could separate the church from any bad apple of a priest, and it ultimately made sense to her, for it was never fair to lump all good in with the bad, was it? By the following spring the two were wed and she was commencing to give birth to her first child.

The Fifth Born would continue to blunder his way through high school, often in trouble, worrying his father and being berated by his mother with more and more vitriol, enough so that The Good Sister, upon witnessing the public shamings at family gatherings, cried for him many nights, but what could she do?

The Deacon had the answer, as always. "Pray," he said, "for his mortal soul."

The day her favorite brother turned eighteen, two months after his high school graduation, her mother ordered him out of the house, to go and make something of himself. For a few nights he slept in the car of his brother, the Fourth Born. When the Good Sister discovered this she fetched him into her own home, but after a couple of days the Deacon put his foot down. The Fifth Born was disrespectful, to him, he said, to the church, to any authority, and his rebellious nature would likely land him in jail, and he was a damn fool to think anything different would come to pass.

The Fifth Born smiled. "Fools are free," he said.

The Fifth Born found his way to the only place that made immediate sense, into the army, Vietnam or no. He served his time without seeing combat and went to college on the GI Bill, having discovered a love of literature in the service, where he thoroughly enjoyed reading books he wasn't forced to read. He spoke with the Good Sister from time to time, giving fair reports of his job as a university instructor, his own family, and any other newsy items of interest, speaking of his love of James Baldwin, John Irving, among many others; but he had little to do with reunions, or baptisms, or family weddings, or confirmations, and kept far from his home town and even farther from the church. "I'm just fine," he would say.

The Good Sister had married well, indeed. The Deacon was a rigid defender of the faith, enforcer of church law, pillar of the congregation. He was a good provider, too, having shrewdly risen through the ranks of a national insurance company. With him she would bear eight children and order the infrastructure of her life toward being a Good Mother, successfully so, by all accounts. She was patient, loving, firm but understanding, and always quick to laugh, even though the Deacon did not share her joyous nature, that shining veneer of her desperation for a peaceful spirit.

When the Fifth Born gave her the news of his divorce, the Good Sister was sorrowful and appalled that her brother's soul was in such grave jeopardy, although the Deacon seemed perfectly smug in informing her that excommunication was a done deal. She did some research and inquiry, however, and learned that the Fifth Born could take a class in the church and ask for special dispensation for good works. It was a chance, at least.

The Fifth Born laughed when she gave him that option. He hadn't been to church since leaving home, which she already knew, of course, and he wondered aloud at her attempt to coax him back into the fold but she pretended not to hear. Sometimes she envied him his freedom, although she was certain the two of them were haunted by shared ghosts and always would be.

The Fifth Born was kind enough not to mention the twisted irony when the Deacon left her. The Deacon's promotion within his company required a move across the country. The Good Sister, though, could not bear to leave her extended family, thought it much too important for her own children to be near them. And that was that. The cold reality that he could so easily leave, however, gnawed at her heart. Her emotions took her to the cusp of that evening when she performed her Holy Communion in the bathroom with the never-closed door shut and locked. But even in the devastating wreckage of marital failure, her children came first, and she would as always tend to them with affection and warmth and humorous support.

She would seek the advice of the Young Father at St. Mary's, attend Mass, volunteer, and kiss her Rosary beads as she dutifully prayed her "Our Fathers" and "Hail Marys." And she would find her way into the confessional booth, curtains drawn, and pour out her petty flaws and dismal failures and any mortal sins that might be obstacles on her path to penance. But she could never, ever, put into words how she had forsaken her beloved Fifth Born, the mischievous boy of her heart. He was a stubborn reminder that this shoddy faith of hers hung on a clerical collar blackened with abandonment, deceit, and the kind of hollow lies she told herself every day, a solitary Mobius Strip of penitence that was destined to spiral on, into the Mysterious Forever.

Acknowledgments

Much gratitude to the breath of fresh air that is River's Edge Media and the guru of How to Treat Writers, Kerry Brooks; to my first editor and husband, Joe Formichella, who sees so well through the clutter; and to my badass second editor, Wendy Reed, who flinches at nothing while sending hugs. Thank you to Chuck Cannon and his gifted way with titles, never banal, always brilliant; and to Shari Smith, who connects the dots I pretty much always fail to see. Finally, love and RIP Jackson, the big black Zen dawg that kept and, I choose to think, continues to keep the energy on Waterhole Branch in just the right place for creativity to flourish. Black dawg down. Don't move, Jackson.

"Opposable Thumbs," title story, *Opposable Thumbs*, Joe Taylor, executive editor, Livingston Press, Livingston AL, 2001

"Yes, Ginny," *A Kudzu Christmas: Twelve Mysterious Tales*, edited by Jim Gilbert and Gail Waller; River City Publishing, Montgomery AL, 2005

"The Thing with Feathers," *Stories from the Blue Moon Café*, volume IV, edited by Sonny Brewer; Macadam/Cage, San Francisco CA, 2005

"LaPrade," *Penthouse* magazine, December, 1977; *Opposable Thumbs*; Livingston Press, Livingston AL 2001; *The Alumni Grill*, edited by William Gay and Suzanne Kingsbury; Macadam/Cage; San Francisco CA, 2004

Excerpted from *In the Dark of the Moon*, a novel, Macadam/Cage, San Francisco CA, 2005; excerpted in *Men Undressed: Women Writers and the Male Sexual Experience*, edited by Stacy Bierlein, Gina Frangello, Cris Mazza, and Kat Meads; Other Voices Books, Chicago, IL, 2011

"Looking for John David Vines," *Climbing Mt. Cheaha: Emerging Alabama Writers*, edited by Don Noble; Livingston Press, Livingston, AL, 2004

"The Fall of the Nixon Administration," *Stories from the Blue Moon Café*, edited by Sonny Brewer; Macadam/Cage, San Francisco CA, 2002; *The Saints and Sinners Anthology*, edited by Amie M. Evans and Paul J. Willis; Rebel Satori Press, Hulls Cove, ME, 2011

"The Seamstress," *Stories from the Blue Moon Café*, volume II, edited by Sonny Brewer; Macadam/Cage, San Francisco CA, 2003

"All the Way to Memphis," *Delta Blues*, edited by Carolyn Haines; Tyrus Books, May, 2010